A Trust Betrayed

By Frances Chidubem Onaku-Duluora

A Trust Betrayed

© 2022 @ Frances C Onaku-Duluora

ISBN: 9798372472709

All rights reserved.

No part of this publication may be reproduced, stored in a retrieval system or transmitted in any form by any means electronic, mechanical, photocopying, recording or otherwise without prior written permission.

Published in Nigeria by

Nkanemi publishers

Appreciation

To God Almighty for giving me the inspiration to do this. To my dear parents: Sir and Lady F.N. Onaku for their constant encouragement, advice and support. To my sisters: Phyllis and Millicent; my brothers: Valentine, Venatius and Vitalis for their concern and prayers. To my dear husband for his loving support, numerous sacrifice and understanding.

CHAPTER ONE

Emeka anxiously searched for her among the people coming out from the arrivals lounge. He became worried as more people trooped out and yet no sign of her. "Does it mean she has been delayed?" He wondered.

"Mekus, ol' boy". Someone said and feeling a clap on his shoulders, he turned to behold an old school mate.
"Jake!" he exclaimed in surprise. "Where did you spring from?" Jake laughed, "Waiting for someone?" He asked.
. "Oh... yes" Emeka answered and turned back to the plane to notice that all the passengers had disembarked. Really worried now, he looked across the tarmac at the few people still scattered around, some anxiously looking out for familiar faces of relations and friends. That was when he saw her approaching, looking out for him. His heart leapt a bit and he excitedly started waving his hands. Jake was completely forgotten. She wore a knee-length red dress which clung to her like a second skin. It showed off her excellent shape, exposing her long well shaped legs which ended up in a red pair of high-heeled shoes made of velvet. Dangling from her ears were a pair of gold earrings. Her beautiful face broke into a lovely smile on noticing Emeka. As he gazed at her, he became more determined that this was the woman he would spend the rest of his life with. He kept staring into her large pair of eyes encased in an oval face which led to a pointed nose tapering off in a well shaped mouth with thin lips. Her long neck makes her look graceful whenever she turns her head.

"Welcome darling", Emeka cried as she went directly into his arms. "I missed you so much, honey", she cried holding him tight as if he would disappear into thin air if she let go.
"Me too", said Emeka. She had travelled to London to be a chief bridesmaid for her best friend in her wedding.
"Hei! I'm still around", Jake reminded Emeka who suddenly remembered that he was still standing there. He gently disentangled himself from her and introduced them.
"Jake is an old school mate", he explained to her. "We attended the same secondary school". "My fiancé", he told Jake. Both of them shook hands. "It's a pleasure". They uttered.

"Congrats man", Jake continued. "She's a beauty! But then you've always been a lucky man ever since I've known you way back". "Thanks Jake". Emeka replied. "But are you trying to tell us that you're the unlucky one?". He teased him.

"It's true you know". Jake insisted. "Remember how you used to play all sorts of pranks with us, yet excel in the examinations while the rest of us would be complaining during our secondary school days". " He used to amaze us". He told the lady.

"Well, we have to get going. If we stay here listening to Jake, we might never make it to the house tonight at all." Emeka said jokingly . "Come and have a drink with us Jake. We need to catch up on old times." He invited. "Oh....no, no I shouldn't intrude. Both of you should catch up first. We'll do ours later." Jake protested.

"No, we wouldn't mind." The lady said. "You'll be most welcome". She assured him.

"Okay then, can't resist a pretty lady's hospitality, but I assure you it'll be snappy." He agreed.

"That settles it then", Emeka said and they all moved towards the car park. Jake came with his, so he followed them behind.

Emeka's house was situated in a low density area of Ikeja. It was a modern bungalow, painted in cream colour and roofed with red alumaco type. The building consisted of five bedrooms, each ensuite, a large sitting room, spacious kitchen. The compound was large and surrounded by a high fence topped with wires of electric protector for privacy. The sitting room was tastily and modestly furnished with modern electrical gadgets and furniture.

"Wao! Mekus, you've arrived". Jake exclaimed. "You have a beautiful place here".

"Let's just thank God for it all". Emeka replied.

"Infact you've got it all. A comfortable home, a beautiful fiancée.......and a good job I know. Well done!" Jake commended him.

"Well, I can't complain, thanks". Emeka replied.

"Wow!"

"Enough of the praises Jake, so what are you having? There's wine, beer, stout. Make your pick".

"A cold bottle of beer would be ok".

The lady had already gone inside to freshen up and as Jake and Emeka relaxed, each with a cold bottle of Star larger beer, chatting over old times, the phone rang. Angel, on coming into the parlour just then, picked it up.

"Hello..."

"Good evening. Please is that Barrister Emeka Ngene's house?"

"Yes."

"Can I speak to him?"

"Sure". She said and handed over the phone to Emeka who had moved nearer, knowing the call was for him and remembering that his mobile phone needed to be charged.

"Hello". He said into the mouth piece.

"Good evening". A deep strange voice boomed at the other end.

"Good evening". He answered back.

"Barrister Ngene?"

"Speaking".

"This is Inspector Okoye of the C.I.D, Ajao Estate branch".

"Is there a problem?" Emeka asked wondering what his involvement with the police was. As far as he was concerned, he had no case with them now.

"There's been a murder". The Inspector continued.

"So...?"

"The deceased is a relation of yours, Nnamdi Ngene".

"W-H-A-T!" Emeka shouted into the phone.

Jake and the lady both started, and on seeing Emeka's face, rushed to him.

"Get yourself together and come down to the station to identify the body". The inspector was still talking.

"I'll be right there". Emeka replied, not believing this was actually happening. Turning slowly towards the lady, "Nnamdi is dead". He said, still in shock and was forced to get a hold on himself as she swooned and fell into his arms in a faint.

CHAPTER TWO

Her name is Angel and she looks like one. That was what attracted Emeka to her in the first place. The innocent look on her face which makes you feel you can trust her in any situation. He had just got out of a relationship in which he had felt stifled and trapped all along. The lady in question wanted him to marry her at all cost and he just wasn't ready to spend the rest of his life with her. Life would be so boring, he thought. As a girl friend, she was okay but as a wife? No way. I need a woman who is sharp and can think fast, not one as dull as ditch water who I have to make all her decisions for. Nneka, the lady was too pliant for her own good. She could never say "no" to anything or offer any reasonable advice or suggestions if approached. All her decisions had to be made by someone. She was too dependent. He needed someone that could think for herself as well as give him words of advice when needed. However Nneka held on like a leech refusing to let go until he had to devise a way to send her packing.

He could still remember that night when he called her into his room and told her that he just found out that his blood genotype was 'AS' which was a lie, but knowing fully well that hers was 'AS' he had to find a way to get her out of his life.

"As you know we're not getting younger". He had started. "One has to start thinking of settling down. And since we're both 'AS" genotype, I'm afraid we have to call it quits as there's no way we can both get married to each other". He had paused. "It would be a disaster because there will be a probability of us having a child who is 'SS'. i.e suffering from sickle cell anaemia which means the red blood cells which carry oxygen around the body develop abnormally. Rather than being round and flexible, they become crescent-shaped which will be resulting in frequent 'crisis' for the child as these abnormally shaped cells have a shorter life span and should be frequently changed". He had explained. We wouldn't want that punishment for any child so it's better we split up now so as not to limit our chances of meeting the right person." He gently told her. Nneka, after crying for she really loved Emeka, agreed that it was for good. Emeka assured her that they would still be friends. He even remembered shedding a few tears himself to make the whole story look real. He allowed himself a little smile now as he recollected the whole episode. The next day, Nneka had packed and gone and he had heaved a huge sigh of relief.

He was just about to retire for the night when his door bell rang and he went to dismiss whoever it was. Greg, his boisterous friend bustled into the house.

"Greg, by this time?" He asked, looking at the wall clock. It was 10pm.

"Mekus ol' boy, you mean you don't know what is happening in town?" Greg asked.

"Has the Saviour himself come down?" Emeka was sarcastic.

"And I'll bother myself looking for you when I would be seriously trying to acquaint my self with Him, trying to save my lost soul". He gushed laughing.

"Then what is worth knowing that can be happening in town?"
"Your favourite stars, your idols: P-square is in town". Greg announced enthusiastically.

"You mean Peter and Paul Okoye?

"The duo and only!"

"Wao! When are they performing?"

"This night. Show starts by midnight. That's why I'm here because I know a workaholic like you wouldn't know".

"Hope they've not taken all the V.I.P's? Emeka asked.

"That's why I came to you now, because I know with your connection, I'm covered".

"Make some calls man". Greg pressed.

"Where's the venue?" Emeka asked.

"Sheraton hotels and towers".

Half and an hour later, they were on their way to Sheraton in Emeka's posh red Rav 4 toyota jeep. On reaching, they were led to two seats in the V.I.P section. It was during the performance which was so thrilling that Emeka noticed the beautiful lady sitting almost adjacent to him on his right side. He wondered why he hadn't noticed her before. She just had to be noticed. She was so entranced by the performance on stage that she seemed hardly aware of any other person around. Emeka suddenly developed divided attention and almost forgot what he came to the place for.

"Greg!" He said, touching him. "Just look at that piece of beauty over there." He enthused. Greg who was so enthralled with the performance dragged his eyes reluctantly from the stage to glance at the object of Emeka's interest.

"Yeah!" He agreed, and sensing where Emeka's interest was heading, continued "But hands off man". He warned his friend.

"Who said I'm already laying my hands?" Emeka asked, but after a thought, "And why the hands off anyway?". He asked.

"She's not for the likes of you? Jake advised him, "Can't you see she's too sophisticated? Moreover, for her to be in the V.I.P, she must be well connected, if you get my drift." He explained on.

"Well, well, well, Greg you always jump to conclusions." Emeka said disgustedly. "When has it become a crime to know the people that 'be' or to look good? She looks quite innocent to me". He defended her.

"Looks can be deceptive you know. Please let's not forget what we're here for'. And saying that he turned his utmost attention back to the stage. Emeka found out he could not concentrate anymore. He found himself in a dilemma. I must get that lady. He thought. But how? He wondered. Well, no Jupiter will stop me. He said determinedly. So engrossed was he with the lady that he didn't know when the first half of the show ended until people started clapping. At that particular time, the lady seemed to be aware of other people in the room and it just happened that immediately she turned to look around, she met Emeka's stare. Not surprised, she smiled at him. Emeka, feeling as if he was floating on air stupidly smiled back. He was completely bewitched. Greg, on seeing that his friend had become hooked, shook him out of his reverie.

"My God", he stared at Emeka, "Don't tell me you've let that lady do a terrible number on your heart." He teased, stealing a glance in the lady's direction. But she had already turned her attention to the young man by her side and seemed to have forgotten all about Emeka.

"I told you." He said triumphantly. "Can't you see she's not alone? He continued, with reference to the young man chatting with her.

"Greg", Emeka looked at him wildly, "I must get her". Greg, who was about to say something stopped on seeing the look on his face. This is serious. He thought. After staring at him for some seconds, he turned back to the stage having concluded that Emeka was crazy.

     The second half of the performance started and all attention went back to the stage. It was so thrilling that even Emeka enjoyed it, though half of his mind was still with the girl. At the end of the performance, everybody scurried for the doors with the result that Emeka lost the girl. However, as luck would have it, just as he came out of the sliding doors of Sheraton, he saw her leaning against a pole. Quickly, he excitedly nudged Greg and pointed towards her. Greg, by now had seen that Emeka was too fast, had no choice but to encourage him, after all it was a game of chance, either he gets her or he doesn't.

"Now is your chance, Mekus. Seems she's waiting for you, but please make sure you come back in one piece. I'm not really in the mood for running around for a hospital this night. I'll be on my way, Goodluck and goodnight.." With that, he started walking towards the car park. Gathering enough courage, Emeka started moving towards the lady who smiled at him in recognition as he approached. Emeka was encouraged, "Hello, waiting for someone?" he asked her with a smile as well.

"No, actually, I'm thinking of a way to get home", she answered.

"Oh! Come on, I'll give you a lift. It's no problem.

"Thank you", she answered, but I wouldn't want to inconvenience you, besides I don't really know you". She politely declined.

"C'mon", he urged. " It wouldn't be an inconvenience". Emeka assured her, "Besides we can only get to know each other through interaction". He joked. Seeing she was smiling at the joke, " I'm clean and you're very safe with me". He assured.

"Ok, what can I say?" she said.

"So, is that a yes?" Emeka asked still not sure of what she meant since she still stood there.

"Well, I can hardly say no", and with that she followed him.

"I'm Emeka". He began, by way of introduction as they walked.

"I'm Angel". She said.

"You sure look like one". Emeka thought she was joking, but she just smiled but said nothing. She seemed to be always smiling, Emeka noticed and was becoming more smitten. They reached the car and both piled inside.

He dropped her. "I musn't forget to thank Greg for taking me to Sheraton this night.

That was how their relationship started.

CHAPTER THREE

Jake drove the three of them to the police station at Ajao Estate since it seemed Emeka was in no shape to drive and Angel, who still appeared shaken couldn't be persuaded to stay back and rest after her journey. She insisted on following them. Nobody talked on the way. Everyone was lost in his or her thoughts.

At the police station, they identified Nnamdi's body alright. He was stabbed from the back. The little hole was still soaked with congealed blood. Emeka, who seemed to have regained complete control of himself again, stared at the inspector.

"What actually happened?" He asked.

"At exactly two o'clock this afternoon, there was a phone call, an anonymous caller who informed us of a dead man at No 2 Lakunle street Ajao Estate. Without identifying herself or even giving us an opportunity to ask questions, she dropped the phone. In fact, we almost dismissed it as a mental case but on second thoughts, we decided to go, and on getting there, we met the door closed but not locked. We opened it, entered and met this sight, half on the rug and half on the settee. We've taken finger prints already and they're being worked on at the lab".

Emeka stared at his dead brother remembering the last time they saw each other before the cold hands of death snatched him away through some vicious people. His brother had been in London for the past four years and only came back last year due to the death of their parents who lost their lives in a ghastly motor accident on their way back from their village. Both of them were the only children of their parents and as such, were very close. Emeka, being the younger of the two had always looked up to and admired Nnamdi in everything he did. He was his idol. When Nnamdi left London for a two-year programme in Petrochemical Engineering, he didn't know he was going to survive his absence because they were very close. Nnamdi, it was, who would always pat him on the back in his most depressing moments saying, "Bro, the world is moving on and so are the people in it. You've got to forget about worries and join in the race. C'mon let's go and get rid of the unpleasant past". And saying so, he would drag him up from his seat and they would hit town. The result always left Emeka with a good feeling. It was always good staying with Nnamdi. He was one for the good things of life and would enjoy it to the end.

The last time he saw Nnamdi was just a week before Angel's return from London. Even though they both lived in Lagos, Nnamdi had never met Angel. There was always something preventing both of them from meeting, much to Emeka's displeasure because he would have really liked his beloved brother to meet his precious fiancée. He had gone to Nnamdi's house that evening and met him enjoying a game of football on the television. It was European league match and Emeka knew better than to interrupt him in the middle of a football match. So he had to e exercise patience till the he would be able to get his brother's full attention.

During the half time, "You look so lean". Nnamdi had exclaimed looking Emeka up and down. "What's wrong?" "Don't tell me it's because Angel is not around". He jokingly added.

"Man, I'm missing her so much. I've never been in love like this before". Emeka admitted all too glad to talk about Angel.

"Wao! Can't wait to set my eyes on this creature who has stolen my baby brother's heart". Nnamdi teased.

"You'll love her, no doubt about that". On second thoughts, he added, "Why don't you come with me to the airport to meet her on the day I'm expecting her back". He invited Nnamdi.

"So, when is this BIG day?"

"Exactly a week today. Gosh! I can't wait'.

Looking at his brother, Nnamdi shook his head and smiled.

"Okay, I'll be there with you". He assured him. "Since you have to pass Ajao estate before reaching the airport, just drop in and pick me up. I must meet this angel of love". He joked.

"By the way, what are your plans of settling down?" Emeka asked his elder brother since he had never spoken of a serious relationship.

"Well, this life is too sweet as of now for me to start taking it so seriously, moreover, I haven't yet met any woman with enough charms like Angel to sweep me off my feet in a rush for the altar chanting 'I do'. He finished up with gesticulations and they both burst out laughing. It was always like that with Nnamdi. One could never stay annoyed in his company for long.

However, two days later, he had called Emeka to say that he couldn't make it since something important had cropped up but promised to come later to the house to meet Angel. Emeka had felt so disappointed because he had already told Angel over the phone that Nnamdi was coming with him to the airport to receive her. He remembered how disappointed she had felt when he later told her that he couldn't make it. He knew Angel was also very eager to meet this brother of his who he was always talking about. He had no doubt then that both of them would kick it off immediately, both having very large sense of humour. Suddenly, he was brought back to reality by the police inspector who was assuring him that they would try their very best to bring the culprits to book.

"What's the use?" He asked wearily. "No amount of investigation will bring him back I only want my brother back." He cried.

"Emeka, what are you saying? The police must do their job". Jake admonished him.

"Of course darling, let them do the investigation. I know how hard it is for you now, but at the end, you'll be satisfied knowing that justice has been done. At least you owe Nnamdi that". Angel encouraged him. She has fully recovered from the shock.

"But who would have done this to Nnamdi?" As far as I'm concerned, he had no enemies. He loved this life. He loved everybody. All were his friend". Emeka wondered.

Seeing that he was ready to break down, Jake took him out and then together with Angel, all the necessary arrangements were made and the body was taken to Glory General hospital where he was placed in a mortuary.

CHAPTER FOUR

Ken was getting ready to enter his car when a black sedan swept into the compound. It was a large compound of four duplexes. They were situated two on each side, opposite each other. Each duplex was surrounded by flowers demarcating it from the other. All of them were occupied. There was a family of four made up of a husband, wife and two children, all daughters. They were occupying the building nearer the gate. On their left lived Nnamdi, Emeka's brother. Opposite his house was Ken and his younger brother. On Ken's right, opposite the family of four was a large family of eight: Father, mother, two girls and four boys.

Since Ken wasn't the only occupant of the compound and the driver and his passenger weren't familiar, he continued entering his car only to be stopped by the sedan's horn. He came out and closed the door of his car. Now what? He wondered. He hated going late to work and he was almost late already.

"Good morning sir". The driver greeted. He was a tall, dark man with twinkling eyes and a very white set of teeth in the midst of a dark face. When he spoke, it was as if he was smiling. It must probably be because of the twinkling eyes. He couldn't be more than thirty-two years, he guessed.

"Please we're sorry for the disturbance but we have to do our job". He apologized. Bringing out his I.D card, he waved it at Ken's face and introduced himself, "Detective Jones and this is Kings". He pointed at his partner.

Ken looked at the small man introduced as Kings. Surely the name doesn't suit him, he thought. The man was almost half of Jones in height, light in complexion with a pair of eyes that looked bored all the time. He had a beak-like nose, probably he was mistaken for a hawk during the creation of the nose. The small man took one look at Ken, then faced his hands. Ken had to quickly glance at his hands to make sure they were okay. "Quite weird", he thought, then turning to Jones, "Well, how can I be of help?" he asked since he couldn't fathom what business he had with detectives.

"Yes you can", Jones replied. We're here for the murder of Mr Nnamdi Ngene.

"You mean Engineer Nnamdi, the one that lives there?" He shouted, pointing to the deceased's house in disbelief.

"Yes".

"But he can't be dead, not Nnamdi. I saw him talking to Onyeka's sister yesterday morning". He continued shouting in shock. By now the other occupants of the compound had started coming out gradually on hearing Ken's shout.

"He was murdered in the afternoon, between twelve o'clock and one pm yesterday". Jones patiently explained.

"I can't believe this". Ken shook his head at the others who had come out. Some were crying while others were shaking their heads in disbelief. "Nnamdi was such a dear fellow". Someone muttered.

"Well, good morning ladies and gentlemen", Jones turned to the crowd. "You've all heard what happened to your neighbor and that's why we're here, for investigation, and we'll appreciate all the help you can give us concerning the murder".

"How can we be of help, please?" Mrs Okenwa, red eyed, asked him. "If you don't mind, we would like to ask each of you a few questions".

"It's okay, I'll just call my office". Ken replied. "Nnamdi was like a brother to me and I'm ready to give all the necessary assistance".

They started with Ken after he placed a call to the office informing them that he would be late.

"Where were you between twelve and one p.m yesterday?" Ken thought for a while, remembering that yesterday was a Sunday.

"I was coming back from church with my brother, in fact we were together in my car on the road.

"What church?"

"Assemblies of God at Idowu street, Mafoluku".

"What time does the service normally end?"

"Well, it depends. There's no particular time. Yesterday it was at twelve-thirty pm. I can remember because a brother asked me for the time just as we came out of the church".

"Can you remember the exact time you arrived here?"

"I can't really say. It normally takes me not less than twenty minutes to get back to the house from the church, but we didn't leave the church premises at exactly twelve-thirty pm since there were other cars in the church compound. We had to wait for our turn before we could move out. So I might have spent at least five or ten minutes in the church premises before coming out of there". He patiently explained.

"Did you notice anything amiss when you came back here?

"Like?"

"Any strange thing in the compound, maybe a stranger or strange car?"

"As far as I can remember, nothing".

"Is there any information you might like to give us concerning Nnamdi?" Ken thought for a while scratching his chin in the process. "Well, nothing much except that he was likeable. I can't think of any reason why someone would like to kill him".

"Okay, thanks for your help".

"You're welcome anytime".

Meanwhile, Mr Kings had moved to Nnamdi's house and was looking around the area. Suddenly, he moved close to Mr Okenwa's eldest daughter who was standing near the house and touched her on the shoulder from the back. The girl screamed and jumped up, then looked back to see the man staring at her hands, she quickly looked at her hands afraid they've developed horns. Seeing nothing amiss, she was about to ask him what it was all about when he suddenly looked at her as if he was seeing her for the first time, muttered "sorry", then moved away. "What a strange man", she thought. "I must be getting jittery. I must get a hold on myself".

Jones moved on to Ken's brother who was told to stay at one end of the compound away from Ken. He confirmed Ken's story but said that later on as Ken was having his siesta and he was watching the telly, a car stopped in front of Nnamdi's house and he saw three men come out of the car but he didn't take much interest in them since he was thoroughly enjoying the film on the television and didn't want to miss any part. He wouldn't even be able to identify the men because he didn't see their faces, but the car was a dark, red Nissan laurel, he volunteered.

Dr Amaechi of the family of six was away with his wife and the last three kids on a short vacation so it was just the eldest son, Onyeka, Ben, the second son and Nkechi, the third child and first daughter. Nkoli, their house-help was also around. Onyeka was the next person Jones moved onto. He was a young man of twenty four and had just finished from medical school. He was doing his housemanship. He was the serious type. His parents knew that his being around meant the house was in capable hands. He would see that everything was done at the right time.

"Your name please?" Detective Jones began.

"Onyeka Amaechi".

"Still in school?"

"Doing my housemanship".

"Oh! A medical doctor". He congratulated him by shaking hands with him. "I admire young, promising people". He told him. He liked putting people at ease in the process of his work.

"Actually, have you noticed anything amiss around here recently?" He began.

"Well, I don't usually come outside, I'm more of an introvert." He started. "But on Thursday evening, at about 5pm, two young ladies, both were tying scarf and holding what looked like the Holy Bible came and asked for 'Brother Nnamdi Ngene'. I was standing right in front of our house waiting to take my younger sister to the market to pick a few items. It was strange to me because I knew Nnamdi was vehemently against this church fanatism to the extent of becoming a "brother'. Strange things do happen, I could remember thinking.

"Seems you were close to him as to know his feelings towards such...."

"Actually, we were good neighbours. There's nobody here that will tell you that he wasn't close to him because he had a way of bringing himself so close to you that you can't shake him off, not that you'll like to, anyway. He was such good company".

"So, did the ladies see him?"

"Ummm, that, I don't know because immediately after showing them his house, my sister came out and we drove off".

Can you describe them?"

"Well, one was very pretty; even though she had her hair all covered with a scarf, I could still detect her beauty. She was slender and tall. She had on a long black skirt and a blue shirt which wasn't tucked in. I think I can identify her if I see her again because I kept staring at her. She is quite light in complexion with a beauty spot between her left nostril and mouth. The other lady is quite ordinary. I noticed her because she was the one that asked the question. She is dark, slender as well, but a bit shorter than the other one. She had on a long, red gown".

"Apart from that, did you notice any other strange happenings here?"

Onyeka shook his head in the negative.

"Where were you between one o'clock and two on Sunday?"
"Inside the house watching Euro sports. I don't normally miss it unless it's inevitable".

"So, you heard nothing at all?"

"Like........?"

"Any unfamiliar sound". Sometimes this detective can be over zealous in asking their questions. He silently thought. How can one fully engrossed in a football match be listening for another kind of noise apart from the constant uproar on the field. He wondered.

Aloud, "No, I didn't". He answered.

"What of your brother and sister? Can you account for their movements on that day?'

"I was watching the telly with my brother while my sister had gone to the saloon from where she informed me that she would visit a friend. She came back later in the evening.

"Do you know whether Nnamdi had any enemy or recently quarreled with someone?"

"No, he didn't look the type to me. He was the jolly type. You can't even imagine him getting angry enough to the point of having enemies".

"That's ok for now. Thanks so much for your help".

"You're welcome".

CHAPTER FIVE

Onyeka's siblings confirmed what their brother said even though they were separately asked. However, none of them noticed anything amiss that day or thereafter. Nkechi told them that she had talked with Nnamdi that Sunday morning. She had come out of the house after dressing up for church and was waiting for her brothers to come down when she saw Nnamdi all dressed and driving out. On passing her, he had teased as usual, "Keche", that was his pet name for her. "Make sure they don't steal you in the church or I would sue everybody there". "You don't want to confirm a date for our wedding". He joked. He was always calling her his wife. She had laughed and asked him where he was going to so early on Sunday morning. It was a few minutes to seven o'clock in the morning. She could remember because they were going for the seven o'clock Holy Mass. He had told her that he was going to church as well and she asked him when he started going to church so early. He had replied that he was going to pray to God to bring back his brother's fiancée safely from London. She had laughed, believing it was one of his numerous jokes. He had waved goodbye and moved on. That was the last she had seen him till now. Asked if she used to visit him at home, she had vehemently shaken her head saying the relationship never reached that extent.

"From your statement", Jones continued, "You said you asked him when he started going so early to church, does it mean he wasn't used to going early to church?"

"Well, I was just teasing him. I don't know if he used to go that early but I've never actually seen him out, so early on Sunday mornings because I'm almost always out by that time waiting for the rest of the family".

"Okay, from the word 'Holy Mass', you attend the Roman Catholic church?"

"Yes".

"And do you know the church Nnamdi attended?"

"I think he was also a Roman Catholic".

"You think?"

"Yes, from some of his utterances".

"Like?"

"Well, as a Roman Catholic, when you talk with one, you'll know immediately".

"Okay!"

"And you didn't happen to have seen him at all in the church that day?"

Shaking her head in the negative, "There are many Catholic churches around, he might have gone to any of them". She answered.

" Okay, thanks for your co-operation".

"You're welcome anytime". She answered.

    Kings who had been standing near Nkoli, Dr Amaechi's house help, suddenly dropped his pen 'accidentally' right in front of Nkoli, and it fell on the ground, almost between her legs. She unconsciously bent down, picked it up and offered it back to Kings who graciously thanked her, noting that she used her left hand.

    Jones moved over to Nkoli. She was a young girl of about fifteen years of age, plumpy and of average height. From her looks, compared with the other three, it seemed she must be devouring the food meant for the four of them. She was fair in complexion, almost escaping albinoism. The first things he noticed on her face were her eyes. They stared piercingly at you as if they were looking right into you. He felt uncomfortable under her stare but braced himself, after all he was a well trained detective who could withstand anything.

"Please, can we know you?"
"My name is Nkoli".

"Nkoli......?"

"Brown".

"What's your relationship with these people?" He asked, pointing at Onyeka and his siblings.

"I stay with them as a house help".

"Did you know Nnamdi?"

"Yes".

"Was he your friend?"

"We were civil to each other. I used to greet him and he would reply back, that's all"

"Do you know the type of friends that used to visit him?"

"No", she replied, avoiding his eyes.

"Why is she avoiding my eyes?" he wondered. Most of these house helps normally know things which are assumed that they don't. He thought.

"Well, did you go to church on Sunday with the others?" He continued.

"No".

"Why?"

"I'm not a Roman Catholic"
"Which church do you attend?"
"I attend Sabbath".

"So you were in, the whole of that fateful day?"

"Yes".

"Before Jones could ask the next question, she suddenly said "I didn't see anything oh".

Ah… what's wrong with this girl? She's behaving rather suspiciously, Jones wondered.

"It's alright, nobody asked if you saw anything". He assured her.

"What were you doing when others were in the church?"

"I was cleaning up the house".

"And…………?"

"I later started cooking lunch."

"Cleaning up the house must have involved sweeping the portion of the compound around your house, I imagine?"

"Yes, but I didn't sweep round the house that Sunday morning".

"Why?"

"Nothing." She adamantly replied while looking down. He stared at her for some moments, then went nearer to her and in a gentle tone, "Look, this is a murder case and it's important that the culprit is known so as to stop whoever it is from committing more." He explained. "We need all the help we can get from you, that is why we're questioning you. It doesn't mean you're the culprit, but if you happen to know something and are hiding it from us, then that makes you an accomplice with the result that if it's found out that you're not telling all you know, you might also be punished by law." He finished.

"I don't know anything". She cried and turning, ran into the house. There goes our number one suspect, he concluded silently. I haven't finished with her yet, he said and turned to continue with his enquiry. He discovered that it was remaining the family of Mr Okenwa who were patiently waiting for their turn. As he started moving towards them to ask if the man of the house would follow him to a corner for questioning, the elder of the two daughters, Sophie suddenly screamed from where she was, "I know who killed Nnamdi. I saw them with my two eyes".

CHAPTER SIX

"Darling, isn't it time you tried getting over Nnamdi's death?" Angel suggested to Emeka when, two weeks after the incident, he was still a shadow of himself. He had lost appetite, his normally immaculate appearance looked unkempt. She had had to remind him yesterday to comb his hair before going to work. Even at work, he couldn't concentrate and had to come back after instructing them on how to discharge their cases for the day. He has his own chambers which he started five years ago but it has become quite popular and he's making a lot of money from it. It's been his pride, but even the thought of going there held no interest for him any more. Infact, he had lost interest in everything. The only reason that keeps him going is his fiancée whose presence has been a great help. I will never stop thanking God for this lady. He thought. Remembering that she asked him a question, "I can't seem to help myself". He answered. "He was the only remaining member of family. He understood me. He made life worth living. My only brother! How can I cope? Who will I turn to in moments of confusion?" he lamented.

"Darl, you have to start from somewhere". She advised him. I know how hard it is for you but I'm sure Nnamdi himself wouldn't have wanted you to grieve so much for him. If you continue this way, you might end up following him to the grave and what happens to your lineage? Your firm is suffering, not to talk of your personality. You've hardly touched food in the past few days. Please Emy, remember that there are other people who still love you so much. I'm always here for you, you know".

    That was when he looked at her and saw that her eyes were filled with tears. He felt really bad that he had let his problems come between them. He remembered that she had borne the worst side of his emotions since he was informed of the murder. He had hardly spoken to her since then except in monosyllables, sometimes ignoring her completely, yet she had patiently borne it all.

"I'm sorry my love". He said as he took her in his arms. "I know I've been pretty difficult and a bit inconsiderate. Please do forgive me".

"There's really nothing to forgive. I understand your feelings but I don't want you to ruin yourself". You have to think of the future". She advised.

"I know but………." Just then the phone rang and he couldn't finish what he wanted to say. He picked it up. It was an unknown number.

"Hello," he began.

"Good afternoon". The voice at the other end answered. "Am I speaking with Barrister Emeka Ngene?" It continued.

"Yes, you are". Emeka answered, hoping it's not another bad news. He didn't think he could cope with more of that now.

"Well, the investigation is in progress. A lady confirmed having seen the people who killed Nnamdi but they're still at large. However, with the description we were given, they were two men. We want to inform you that we're on our way to your house to know how possible it is to get the names of Nnamdi's acquaintances and any other relevant information concerning your brother". Jones enquired.

"Ok, I'm around". Emeka assured him half heartedly. Though he's curious to know who killed his beloved brother and why, this investigation is doing little to console him. "Why, this won't bring Nnamdi back to me. He sadly told himself.

"That's fine. We're on our way". Jones promised him.

"See you then and thanks for the effort".

"It's no big deal. We're only doing our job".

Emeka dropped the phone and turned to Angel who was expectantly looking at him. "That was the detective investigating Nnamdi's death". He explained.

"Have they found out the murderer?" She asked.

"Well, he said somebody claims to have seen them so they're coming over for more information about Nnamdi".

"What is it darling?" He asked her on seeing that she had lost colour and suddenly looked pale.

Recovering fast, "No, it's nothing. I guess it's just the excitement of knowing that the murderer has being found so soon". She quickly explained.

Just then the door bell rang. Did they fly? Emeka wondered since it was not even up to five minutes since he spoke to Jones. On opening the door, Jake sauntered into the house. Jake has been very concerned ever since the incident. He had been phoning almost everyday to know how far the investigation had gone and how Emeka is faring. He took one look at Emeka and whistled. "Man, you sure look finished. What have you been doing to yourself?" he scolded Emeka. "How come you allowed him to degenerate like this?" he admonished Angel.

"Leave her alone. It's not her fault". Emeka defended Angel.

"But just look at you", Jake continued. "You look a shadow of yourself. Good old Nnamdi wouldn't want you to follow him to the grave so soon which is exactly what is bound to happen if you don't get a grip on yourself".

"I've been telling him that". Angel added looking very sad.

"You knew Nnamdi?" Emeka asked Jake due to his earlier 'Good old Nnamdi' pronouncement.

"No, it's just from what I've been hearing about him from people. I've been doing my own private investigations, you know".

"Oh, Jake, we really don't know how to show our appreciation on how concerned you've been ever since this unfortunate situation". Angel said.

Grrr-grrr..., goes the door bell.

"That should be the detectives". Emeka said as Angel went to open the door.

"Which detectives?" asked Jake.

"The ones covering Nnamdi's death". Emeka answered.

Jones and Kings entered and greeted them. Emeka stood up, shook hands with them and introduced Jake and Angel. Jones, on looking at Angel almost had to gape. What a specimen of beauty! He thought. God must have spent an extra day on her. So this man has such treasure well tucked in here. After the introductions, he proceeded in telling them what happened in Nnamdi's compound.

After Sophies's shout, there had been a short silence, then all hell broke loose as everybody hurried to Sophie's side. Her mother, he had remembered had looked at her daughter as if she had gone mad.

"Don't mind her, she doesn't know what she's saying". She hastily told Jones who had reached where they were and was staring at Sophie and the mother. As the mother made to lead her inside the house, she started following, but suddenly stopped and broke away from the mother.

"Mum, please believe me, I'm alright and I know what I'm doing". She assured her mum. Then, turning to Jones. "I said I saw the people that killed him". She maintained, looking so calm. Her sister and the rest of the family were all staring at her in shock. "What's Sophie up to?" Olivia, her younger sister asked herself. What kind of super heroine is she trying to be? If she knew what happened, why didn't she tell anyone, even me? She wondered because they were very close and had no secrets.

Detective Jones had made a sign to Kings to follow them as he led Sophie to a corner of the compound where there could be privacy, politely stopping the girl's mum as she made to follow them.

"Repeat what you said". Jones kindly requested when they were finally alone. When she had said it at first, she had felt very relieved. It was as if a large burden had been lifted from her chest but on seeing her mum's reaction, she had wondered if she was doing the right thing, but it was already too late to back out. Since she had started it, she must complete it.

"I said I saw who killed Nnamdi". She repeated, staring at Jones.

"It's okay, let's start from the beginning". Jones kindly told her.

"Your name......?"

"Sophie OKenwa".

"Student?"

"Yes, three hundred level, at university of Benin."

"What course are you studying?"

"Bio chemistry".

"What was your relationship with Nnamdi?" She became shy all of a sudden and started looking down.

"Was he your boyfriend?" Jones gently asked and she nodded, still looking down.

"Okay, tell us what happened". He persuaded before she clams up.

All this time, Kings was just staring at her. This man makes me uncomfortable, she thought. Deciding to ignore him, she turned her full attention on Jones who at this particular period seemed so kind and understanding.

CHAPTER SEVEN

"I had visited Nnamdi that morning, around 10am. I can remember looking out of the window waiting for him to come back from church because he told me the previous day that he would attend the Holy Mass the next day since he had started having a feeling of being closer to God. I had discovered that I was pregnant for him for sometime but didn't have enough courage to tell him because I didn't know what his reaction would be. You see, I loved him very much and didn't want to loose him. So when he said he was going to try and start going to church, I was happy because I felt that he was becoming quite serious in life. I then gathered enough courage to go and tell him that Sunday.

Already I felt that since he had started thinking of getting closer to God, he wouldn't be so harsh if things turned sour. Moreover, for him to think that way, it meant he was becoming more serious in life and might see this as a better opportunity of settling down".

"At a quarter to ten o'clock, I saw his car coming into the compound from the window where I was watching out for him, I could remember that my heart flew into my mouth but I gathered enough courage to move on. I also had to hurry up because he told me the previous day that he had an appointment at twelve o'clock that Sunday, after which he would go to his brother's place at Ikeja to welcome his fiancée who was due back from London that same day. When I got there, he was pleased as usual to see me. In fact, throughout our relationship I had never seen him annoyed for more than one second. He was too good natured for that kind of feeling. Well, he had already changed because he was dressed in a red T-shirt and a pair of black, stripped shorts. That was how he used to relax at home". Jones remembered that that was the same dressing the man had on him when he was discovered.

I sat down and we started gisting. He excitedly went on telling me about the sermon the Reverend Father had given. In fact, one could see that he was inwardly pleased with himself and that the decision he took to go to church was the best thing to happen to him. I was happy for him too and didn't know how to tell him what was on my mind without spoiling the happiness radiating from his face. We talked for about one and a half hours. Nnamdi was never tired of talking. After sometime, I became pressed and excused myself to go to the toilet.

Just as I was entering the toilet, the door bell rang. When I came out of the toilet, I could hear voices. I tiptoed to Nnamdi's room upstairs to see the people through the close circuit T. V. in his room. From there you could see all that is going on in the sitting room. You see, nobody knew of my relationship with Nnamdi, not even my sister. The whole thing was a secret because I didn't know how my parents would have taken it had they known about it. So I wanted to be sure of who was there first before coming out but what I saw when I looked in the circuit shocked the hell out of me and scared me out of my wits. Nnamdi was on his knees, looking very scared. I could see his face clearly because he was facing the circuit. Backing me were two men who were dressed in black from head to toe. One of them, the smaller one was holding what looked like a long knife with very sharp edges in his left hand. It was glinting. I couldn't hear what they were saying even though it appeared he was being told something by them. The smaller of them suddenly turned his face. I don't know why he did it, he probably heard a noise but that was to my advantage because it was then I saw his face clearly because he stayed like that for up to five seconds. It is a very beautiful face; too beautiful for a man. He is light in complexion, had a small mustache. I could remember thinking that looked strange on his face but there it was alright. The other man is quite huge but I couldn't see his face very well. He was darker than his partner in complexion. Suddenly the bigger of the two men grabbed Nnamdi's two hands roughly but tightly while his companion dug the knife with all his might into Nnamdi. I could see Nnamdi opening his mouth to scream but the huge man stopped that by stuffing his mouth with a rag which he brought out from his pocket. Nnamdi lay in a pool of blood. As quickly as they entered, they left. I was too terrified to act, and also too confused. If I started screaming, my mum would know I was there and she isn't supposed to know. She would kill me for visiting a bachelor alone in his house, not to talk of the pregnancy. Due to that fear, when I rushed downstairs, I quickly took the back door and left, not to our house but to a nearby call center where I quickly made the call to the police station pleading anonymity. I haven't told anyone yet, not even my younger sister who I'm very close to. I've not had any rest of mind since then. I feel better now though, having told you the whole story." She sighed with relief. Jones and Kings also both started breathing normally again because they've been holding their breaths throughout the story due to fear of interrupting the fragile-looking young lady and end up making her too nervous to continue.

Clearing his throat Jones began his questions,

"How do you know you're pregnant?"

"I've missed my period for two weeks. It used to be so regular" Sophie answered.

"Did you do a pregnancy test?"

"No, I'm too scared to do one."

"Then you can't be too sure that you're pregnant until you perform one". Jones told her.

"For how long has this relationship between you and Nnamdi been going on?" He continued.

She thought for a while, "I think it's been over four months". She answered.

"And you were able to keep it secret all this while?" Jones couldn't believe his ears because he knows how girls like discussing their boyfriends.

"Yes, it was possible because most of the time I'm hardly here. I stay at the campus ,so we kept contact mostly through phones and sometimes, on his way to Enugu for business, he would branch to the school to see me. My parents are very strict regarding relationship with the opposite sex but I couldn't help falling in love, so it was my suggestion that we kept it a secret." She explained.

"While you were at, did Nnamdi have any enemy or is there anyone he recently had a fight with?"

"That's what I've been thinking of. I can't think of him having enemies because everybody liked Nnamdi. He was really lovable, very jovial. But I do remember that he was looking forward to a contract he just got which would earn him millions and he told me that he would give half of it to his colleague who would have won it were he not around a reasonable percentage. It's just to tell you how generous he was. Whoever did this must be a sadist". She concluded emotionally.

"Interesting", Jones intoned. "Do you know who this colleague of his is?" He asked.

Sophie shook her head negatively. Suddenly something occurred to her. "You mean the guy might be his rival at the office since he took what would otherwise have been the guy's possession?" She looked up at him inquiringly.

The lady must, among other qualities, be smart. Jones noticed.

"You're already on the right track to unraveling the case". He assured her.

"However we can't conclude yet. He might be innocent whoever he might be, however we will definitely like to know the guy." He added. "So do you know where he was working?". He asked her.

"ATTAMCO Nig Ltd." She answered. "It's an oil servicing company located at Surulere".

"Any more questions?", he asked Kings who shook his head in the negative.

"Meanwhile don't tell any other person what you told us". He told Sophie, who nodded in the affirmative.

"But what of my parents? What will you tell them?" She asked, looking at Jones anxiously. They'll definitely kill me if they hear I'm pregnant".

"Don't worry, just leave everything to me". He assured her.

CHAPTER EIGHT

There was silence when the detective finished the story. Angel was staring at Emeka to know his reaction. Jake, all through the story was looking at Kings because the guy, at a particular time decided to take such an important interest in his shoulders. He had kept looking sideways to make sure his shoulders were alright and hadn't suddenly grown out of proportion. Finally he broke the silence.

"Are you sure the girl is telling the truth? He asked. "This story looks made up". He concluded.

"Why do you think she would she be lying?" Jones asked him.

"Well, probably to attract a little attention to herself". Jake said.

"You may be right anyway but that's a good start as far as I'm concerned until we hear something contrary to that". Jones told him.

"Well, that's an encouraging story, Mr Jones", Angel said, "However", she continued, "I hope she would be able to identify these people accurately".

"So how can we be of help here?" Emeka asked listlessly.

"Frankly, I don't like how you're taking this. Was this man not your blood brother?" Jones flared at Emeka.

"It's alright Mr Jones", Angel placated him before Emeka could reply. "He's still in shock you know", so we have to take things easy. If there's any way we can help find Nnamdi's murders, we're ready".

"This man doesn't deserve this lady . What a loving, caring and understanding woman". He thought.

"It's just that some dangerous men are still at large somewhere and if not found , might still do more damage." He explained to them.

"If you don't mind", he continued, "We would like to ask you a few questions".

When there was no objection, he turned to Jake,

"So who are you sir?" he asked him.

"I'm just a friend of his". He answered pointing at Emeka.

"Do you know Nnamdi, the dead man?"

"Hardly"

"Meaning....?"

"We never really got the chance to meet except the little I've heard from those who knew him."

"Who and who knew him?"

"Is this some sort of interrogation?" Jake joked.

"Depends on how you see it". Jones matched his attempt at humour.

"But I wouldn't be of much help since I didn't even know the dead guy personally".

"Ok, so who and who knew him then?" Jones repeated his previous question.

After a pause during which Jake seemed to be debating on whether to answer the question or not, he finally made up his mind. Ignoring Jones, he turned to Emeka and Angel, announced his departure and stood up to leave.

"That's an offence that could get you in court mister". Jones calmly told him without looking at him.

"Please Jake, don't take it so hard". Angel pleaded. "They're just doing their job. At least for Emy's sake, why don't you try to co-operate".

Jake looked at her for some minutes, then sat down again.

"Well.......?" He looked at Jones.

"That's my number one enemy in this case", Jones sadly thought.

"So who are your informants?" He continued.

"Emeka and some of Nnamdi's friends I think".

"Those friends have got names I believe?"

"Sure".

"Like to tell us?"

"No!" Jake firmly said. "My God what have I got myself into". He silently asked himself.

"Actually, it's not a question of choice. We want to know". Jones equally insisted.

"Look here friend, I've taken enough of this nonsense. What have you got to do with who I talk to in my private life?"

"Well, I'm sorry if you feel we're prying, but all these are important information which will help us in the investigation and also for your own good. Who knows who will be the next victim? It could be any of us". Jones calmly explained.

"Jake please..." Angel pleaded.

"Mr Schechem". He reluctantly offered. "And I hope you aren't going to embarrass him with these questions you're bombarding me with". He warned them.

"That's for us to decide". Jones answered back.

"So where were you having the discussion?" He continued.

"At a night club". "I might as well resign myself to fate". He decided wordlessly.

"Name please…"

"Jabo-Jabo".

"Which part of Lagos?"

"Surulere".

"How long have you known Emeka?"

"Way back, since secondary school days".

"And you never met the brother?"

"We just met again on the day of murder since we left school. Moreover must I know all the family members even if we've been in contact?" He angrily retorted.

"Who does this man think he is, asking very unnecessary questions and expecting to be answered?". He furiously wondered.

"So describe your meeting on the day of the murder".

"We met accidentally at the airport".

"What do you mean by 'accidentally'?"

"When something happens by chance mister". He sarcastically answered.

"Jake….." It was Angel again.

"If not for this lady…….", Jake sighed. "I was passing by when I saw someone who looked like him and on getting closer, saw it was actually him. Really, it was a pleasant surprise". He smiled remembering their meeting at the airport after so many years.

"I'm sure it was'. Jones added. "So what were you doing at the airport?" he continued.

At this point Emeka who has been watching all the drama expressionlessly, remembered that he didn't even remember to ask Jake what he was doing at the airport. He had been so carried away by Angel that the thought never even crossed his mind.

"I brought a friend who wanted to travel to America".

"What is your relationship with the friend?"

"For God's sake he was just my brother-in-law's friend's son". He was exasperated. "I guess you would also like to know his name, which part of America he was travelling to". He added sarcastically.

"So how do we meet your brother-in-law?" Jones continued ignoring the sarcasm.

"A Mr Spirop residing at Victoria Island. The street's name is Herbert Macaulay Lane but you have to forgive me for forgetting the exact number of the house".

"Thanks for your co-operation although the number of the house would've been very important to us". Anyway, this is probably your first time of being questioned by detectives. In our work, every piece of information is very necessary". Jones explained to him.

It was at this moment that Kings removed his eyes from Jake who heaved a huge sigh of relief. He had been tensed up during the whole interrogation especially with Kings eyes steadily on him.

CHAPTER NINE

"May I know your name lady?" Jones turned to Angel.

"Angel Dakar".

"So what's your relationship with the deceased?"

"He would have been my brother-in-law.

"Do you permanently stay here?"

"No" She shook her head. "Not yet anyway. I'm just here now because of the tragedy that befell Emy". She further explained.

"Home is where then?"

"17 Jumota Street Allen Avenue".

"Alone or with your parents?"

"Really, are all these questions necessary?" She asked, smiling a bit nervously.

"I'm sorry". Jones apologized. "However it's all part of the investigation". He explained.

"It's alright darling. You don't have to answer if you don't feel like it". Emeka chipped in, talking for the first time since they entered. Jones glared at him.

"Well.......?" Jones smiled at Angel, ignoring Emeka.

"It's ok dear. I can handle it". She assured Emeka, then turning to Jones,

"With my parents, Mr and Mrs Dakar". She answered.

"How close were you to Nnamdi?"

"That's more like it". She said softly. "I never met him". She answered.

"Why?" Jones seemed surprised.

Kings, at this point shifted his gaze from her to Emeka, then back at her again. Her heavy sigh of relief stopped half way. The man had been gazing at her since she started being interrogated.

"We never really got the chance to meet which I regret. Something was always cropping up". She sadly explained.

"Something like......?"

She raised her eyes for a while like one deep in thought.

"Okay", she seemed to have remembered something. "Like the day I came back from London. He was supposed to come and meet me at the airport with Emy, but it was later cancelled because another engagement came up". She told them.

"Do you have any idea what the engagement was all about?"

"No! That was just what Emy told me".

"How long has your relationship with Barr. Ngene being going on?"

She looked at Emeka for assistance, but he also appeared to be trying to remember". Finally, she seemed to have calculated it. "About two months". She said.

"So you really don't know anything about the deceased that'll help in the investigation?". Jones looked disappointed.

"I wish I knew'. She said apologetically.

Emeka, at this point remembered that he hadn't offered them anything. "Darling, please do get some drinks for the gentlemen." He told Angel. Jones looked at him in surprise because that was the last thing he expected from him at that moment. "I'll pass". He shook his head.

"I'll have a coke". Kings said. "So the man can talk". Angel thought. She got up and got the coke. On serving him, Kings observed that she used her left hand.

CHAPTER TEN

"Such a charming and lovely lady for a wife". Jones commented as he and Kings were on their way after leaving Emeka's house. "Not to talk of understanding and good manners, she's got them all. Wow! If I had her type in my house, I wouldn't be leaving the home longer than usual". He enthused.
"Who are you talking about?" Kings asked, glancing at him.
Jones looked at him as one gone insane. "Were there two women in that house?" He angrily asked him.
"Oh! You must mean, ehm........, what's her name again?"
"Angel". Jones almost shouted at him, wondering which game his partner was up to. The lady's beauty is obvious to everybody except a blind person. Kings can't say he didn't notice that.
"Angel, yes". Kings drawled smiling. "Well, I only saw a lady with anxious eyes". He continued. "About the charming aspect, I must confess I didn't notice". He finished.
Such a weird man, thought Jones. But then, he has always been the expert in

unraveling such mysteries and that's why he's so dependable. However, he's being grossly unfair to the lady in this matter. When you see something good, it wouldn't harm to admit it. He silently admonished.

"Of course she would be worried. Who wouldn't? " he barked at Kings. "The murdered man was to be her brother-in-law and her fiancé doesn't seem to be handling the loss well". He continued. They had faced Emeka after, but all he could answer when he was asked if he knew of Nnamdi having anyone with a grudge, was that he wasn't aware of any. Before they could further question him, he had broken down and wept bitterly. They had been embarrassed, but Angel assured them that it was a positive reaction since that was the first time he had done that since Nnamdi's death.

"C'mon what's the meaning of this?" Jake had bellowed. "Be a man Emeka. This isn't the end of the world. Why don't you get a grip on your self". He had admonished Emeka. Then he, politely but firmly asked the detectives to excuse them.

"We'll be back". Jones had said and they left with Jake glaring at them.

"What do you think of Jake?' he asked Kings, as an afterthought.

"He seemed very worried and ill at ease". Kings answered without hesitation.

"Well, even though he is a bit hot tempered, he seems to be a loyal friend considering the fact that he and the barrister had not been in contact in a long while only for the disaster to occur on the very day they met again by chance; yet he seems so concerned". Jones narrated. Kings had no reply for that.

Two days later, Jones had a call from Sophie's mum who was in a panic.

"They want to kill my daughter". She wailed into the phone.

"Who wants to kill your daughter?" Jones asked

"I don't know. Please come". She pleaded.

"Okay, I'll be there as soon as I can". He promised.

Sophie had been called to identify some suspects but she couldn't identify any of the people she saw among those gathered. She hadn't even seemed scared at all. Infact the girl had been so co-operative. He really felt sorry for her. Such a beautiful young lady to have got herself involved in all this. He had vowed to do all in his power to protect her. As for the pregnancy, she hadn't gone to see a doctor yet. She's so scared, she had admitted when he asked her why she hadn't gone yet. So he had promised to take her there himself on Saturday. Today is just Thursday. He told himself. "What has upset the mother so much?" he wondered. She had sounded almost hysterical. He decided to call on Kings to accompany him to the house.

Emeka had just come back from work when his phone rang. On picking the phone, he found out that it was Jake.

"Ol, boy, what's happening?" Any news yet? Jake asked sounding too excited that Emeka had to wonder if he was a bit drunk. Angel had left that morning after seeing that he had become a bit better. Really, he felt much better after the breakdown in front of the detectives. He now felt ready to face the world and help to unravel the mystery surrounding the death of his beloved brother. "God help those murderers if found. I would personally deal with them".He had said to himself.

"Nothing has been heard". He answered Jake.

"What of Angel?" He sounded even higher.

"She's at her parents". Emeka answered. "What's with you man? Are you drunk or what?" He asked Jake a little confused. Emeka, being a straightforward person and not one for pretences had to ask. Jake piped down immediately."No, I'm not drunk". He answered. "I didn't even know I was sounding abnormal". He apologized.

"You were sounding like someone that won a jack pot". Emeka told him. Jake started laughing.

"Anyway, how're you doing yourself?" He asked.

"I'm alright. It's just that I miss Angel. I wonder why she hasn't called yet. She promised to call once she reaches home, but I'm yet to hear from her. He worriedly complained.

"I'm sure she must have a cogent reason. That lady is crazy about you, you know". Jake assured him.

"I know. The feeling is mutual". Emeka agreed.

"I've got to go. I just called to know how things are going. Whether there is any development in the case and to know how're doing".

"How do I thank you Jake for your concern?"

"Oh! It's nothing. What are friends for? Just don't forget to inform me of any development". He reminded Emeka.

"I won't. I'm grateful".

"Ok, take care then".

"Yeah, you too".

"Bye".

"Bye". He dropped the phone and was just about to enter the room to change his clothes when the phone rang again. It was Angel.

Mrs Okenwa opened the door to admit Jones and Kings. She was looking worried. "Thanks so much for coming so soon". She told them. "I've always known that girl would be the death of me". She continued. "Imagine getting herself involved in a police case". She lamented.

"It wasn't her fault, moreover it was quite brave of her to have opened up. Not everybody would do that". Jones defended Sophie.

"Well, if you say so". Sophie's mum told them.

"So what exactly happened?" He asked.

"Yesterday afternoon", Mrs Okenwa started; "A certain Mike came looking for Sophie. He said he was her course mate in school and wanted to borrow a note from her. Luckily, she wasn't around so I told him to come back this morning to see her. When my daughter came back, I gave her the message. She was surprised because she didn't know any Mike in her class and she said that her only course mate that lives around is a girl. That was when I became scared, so when he called again this morning, I told him that unfortunately for hin, Sophie had to rush out in the early hours of the morning for an important engagement and that she wouldn't be back early. As he was going, I told Sophie to look through the upstairs window to know if she knew the man. She looked and told me that he wasn't her course mate but that his movement looked familiar. She thinks she had seen him before. I then became more worried and that was when I decided to call you". She ended.

"Can she remember where she had seen him before?" Jones asked.

The woman shook her head saying the daughter couldn't remember.

"Did you tell the man to come back again?"

"No, but he said he might check again".

"Is she in?"

"Yes, since the latest incident, I've kept her indoors. Please can I request for police protection?" She wailed.

"We'll see what we can do about that". He promised.

"I think we would like to......." He didn't finish his statement as Sophie burst into the room shouting, "Mum, mum, I think I can now remember where I've seen that man". She announced, then stopped short on seeing the detectives.

"Where, please?" Jones seized the opportunity immediately. He had been about to ask if they could see her just before she ran into the room.

Turning to him, she looked straight at him, "That was the man, the huge one who tied the rag round Nnamdi's mouth to prevent him from screaming after he was stabbed.

"Hello darling". It was Angel.

"Darling!" Emeka exclaimed. "What's wrong? You didn't call as promised. Hope all is well dear".

"Not really well". Angel replied. "My mum isn't well. She just came back from the hospital".

"Oh! So sorry dear. What's wrong with her?"

"They said she has typhoid fever and malaria, but she's much better now. We were all worried but thanks be to God it didn't take a turn for the worse."

"I'll be on my way to see her then".

"No dear, that's not necessary though it's quite nice and thoughtful of you, but the doctor said she needs a lot of rest and shouldn't be disturbed. So it's all lots of sleep for her. Don't worry, I'll come tomorrow. I miss you so much". She assured him.

"Same here love. Are you sure I shouldn't come over?". He insisted.

"No, it's alright. Don't bother, ok. I know you care. Meanwhile, is there any progress in the investigation?"

"I've heard nothing. Jake just called some minutes ago. He asked of you".

"Oh, that's nice of him. You've got a friend there".

"Yes, he's a good one". He affirmed.

"Well, I've got to go. See you tomorrow".

"See you, give my love to mum".

"I will honey".

"Love you".

"Love you too". And she hung up.

CHAPTER ELEVEN

The sliding glass doors of JABO JABO night club swung open admitting two men; one was tall and the other smaller. The latter looked around with rather bored eyes. The taller of the two walked straight to a bar, sat on a stool and requested for a glass of scotch. From where he was sitting, he surveyed his surroundings. The room was large and air-conditioned. At one end was a dais on which a band of five men played expert swing. Around the room were tables and chairs. The dance floor took up the major part of the room. There were about ten couples on the floor dancing to the light music. In a big alcove opposite him, a number of girls sat at tables chatting with the incessant noisy volubility of magpies. Well dressed people kept coming in. Most of them preferred to sit at the tables drinking and listening to the band. "This is a rich man's club", thought Jones. Kings, after surveying the place too while standing, walked up to join Jones at the bar. Bringing out his I.D card, he shoved it under the bar man's nose and asked for Mr Schechem. The man looked harried.

"Please I think this is a case for the manager". He said.

"Ok then, so how do we see him?" Jones asked.

The man looked at his watch, it was just a quarter past nine o'clock.

"He's not around yet; but I can assure you that he'll be here by ten o'clock sharp. He normally keeps to time".

Jones and Kings exchanged glances. "We'll wait". Jones said.

Meanwhile the club was filling up. More people were coming in. A group of people suddenly entered. They were five in number: three whites- two men and a woman, two blacks-a man and a woman. They chose a table in the center of the room. The black man looked familiar. On closer look, they recognized Jake. His companions were all engrossed in what they were discussing. A waiter appeared at their table to take orders.

"Can you recognize the demonstrator?" Jones asked his partner.

"That's Jake". Kings answered without removing his eyes from the group. Jones noticed the black lady among them. She was exceptionally pretty, he noticed, even though half of her face was covered with a pair of large black shades. She had on a wig or weave- on, he couldn't decipher and a beauty spot just under her nose. She wasn't talking much, but kept up a steady smile on her face. She seemed a bit familiar to him and he couldn't get himself to remember where he had seen her before.

"What about the lady? She looks a bit familiar too?" He asked Kings.

Just then, the bar man signaled them that the manager was around. Taking one more look at the lady, Jones joined Kings who was already on his way towards the direction pointed out to them.

"Hello….Can I help you?" The club manager asked them after they had seated themselves. Kings observed the room they had just entered. It was a large office whose floor was completely covered with brown ceramic tiles. A large table stood in the middle behind which an elderly man of about fifty years sat and peered at them through a pair of thick glasses. He was black in complexion with such bushy hair that seemed a pair of scissors hadn't met for many years. But it was neat and well kept, giving him the appearance of men of the stone ages. He was a little on the slim side with very tiny pair of eyes, a wide nose and a pair of thick lips.

"Yes, you can sir". Jones answered him. He showed the man his I.D card, "Detectives from the police force investigating the death of a man who we believe was an acquaintance of a member of your club".

"So how can I help?"

"We would like to talk to your club member but unfortunately we don't have his contact information, so we would like you to get that from you". Jones patiently explained.

The man looked at them thoughtfully, considering what he had just been told. Finally, he told them that it was unprofessional and a breach of trust to give out his members contact details, "But however since it's a murder case and you are the law itself, I guess I have no choice but to co-operate". He concluded and pressed a bell. A young boy of around sixteen years old, smartly dressed in thickly starched and well ironed uniform of white shirt, tucked into a red pair of trousers; complete with a red bow tie and a pair of highly polished black shoes that one could see his image on that pair came in.

"Please bring the membership book". The manager requested without glancing at him.

"Yes, sir'. The boy answered and stepped out. He was back before before one could blink an eye. On one side of the giant sized grey book, MEMBERS OF

JABO-JABO was scrawled in silver letterings.

"Thank you". The manager told him and the boy disappeared.

"The man's name?" he requested.

"Mr Schechem".

He browsed through the book turning to the 's' section. "There are two Schechem's here". He observed. "Give us both addresses. The rest is our headache". He was told.

The man wrote both addresses on a piece of paper which he tore from a note pad.

"This is between you and I". he told them.

"Don't worry, we won't betray your confidence". Jones promised him.

Coming back into the main reception of the club, they noticed that Jake and the black, pretty lady were not among the now, small group on the table. Kings looked round and saw them dancing. It was a quarter past eleven o'clock pm, so they decided to be on their way.

"Are you ready Olivia?" Sophie called out to her younger sister? They were both going shopping. Since the incident of the false course mate, she was never allowed to go out alone even though she has two policemen with her.

"Almost...", shouted her sister from her room.

"Wow! Are we going for a party?" Sophie teased her sister on coming into her room. It was typical of Olivia to always appear in her very best whenever she's going out, whether casually or not, unlike Sophie who rather prefers looking simple most of the time.

"Well, you never can tell who we're going to meet". Olivia teased back while applying some final touches to her make-up. "Actually, you don't have to worry much, that hunk of a detective is already head over heels in love with you". She added smiling knowingly at her sister.

"Which hunk of a detective?" Sophie was non plussed, starring at her sister. Frankly, she couldn't understand what she was talking about.

"Which one among those two detectives is the hunk huh? Don't pretend you haven't noticed it". She added on seeing the look on Sophies's face. "Anyway", she continued, "That guy is crazy about you. When you're around, he can't keep his eyes off you. Moreover, look at how fast he arranged for police protection for you. Never knew that was possible in this country. Barely two hours after they left, he arrived back here with two policemen. Mehn, if I can find someone that can care like that for me, what else would I want?"

"Hei! OLIVIA, you're always reading false meaning into things. Will you ever stop?

The guy is only doing the job for which he's paid".

"He's over doing it then. You know what I'm saying is true. You just don't want to agree with me".

"*A-beg,* let's go jare. You romantic soul." Sophie said and got up from the chair shaking her head. Olivia has always been an emotional type and a true romantic. She thought; moreover these romance novels she reads are not of help at all. They entered the car. Olivia sat in front with the driver while Sophie sat at the back between her police escorts.

'G-r-r-r-ring...', the door bell rang. Mrs Schechem opened the door of their flat in Festac town to two gentlemen.

"Good morning ma". Jones greeted. "Is this Mr Schechem's house?" he asked.

"Yes, it is". She answered.

He brought out his I.D card and stated their mission.

"Please do come in". she invited them.

"You said my husband knew the deceased?" she asked when they had all seated.

"Probably..... We're not sure yet. That's why we would like to see him".

"I'm sorry, my husband is not in town right now. He's in U.S. and is expected back in two weeks time.

The two men exchanged glances at each other.

"Do you know a certain Engr Nnamdi Ngene?" Jones asked after a moment.

The woman shook her head.

"What of Mr Jake?" The woman repeated the gesture.

Having got nothing encouraging, they thanked her and stood up with a promise from her to help in anyway she could whenever it's possible. They left their complimentary card with her. At the second Schechem's house, they were told he had left for work, however the niece who met them directed them to his office at Surulere.

"I hope we'll get him at the office". Kings wished, looking at his wrist watch which read a quarter to nine o'clock.

"We can always wait for him to come back later". Said Jones.

"What do you think of what the young lady said about her visitor?" Kings asked.

"You mean Sophie?"

"Yes".

Jones thought a for a while, "It probably means the killers have got some information about her presence on that fateful day and also want to eliminate her, or it might just be a coincidence". He answered.

"Which makes me wonder if she's still suffering from shock and in the process likens everyone to the killers". Kings wondered aloud.

"That may be so, but then she doesn't strike me as somebody who will say something she isn't sure of". Jones hotly defended her.

Kings glanced at Jones, but said nothing. It looks like he is developing a soft spot for that lady judging from the way he's always defending her. Also the urgency with which he got police protection for her made him gasp. What normally takes at least one whole day, sometimes even two due to the necessary protocols involved, took him just a few hours and he was really frantic until it was achieved. Well, it's not my business, he thought but Jones has to be careful. It wouldn't do for him to get involved with a witness in this case since everybody is a suspect until proven innocent. He looked at Jones again.

"So, how is she fairing with her protection?" He asked Jones.

"I saw her yesterday. She's okay". He replied, remembering how he had gone to see her on impulse. He was always looking for an excuse to see her nowadays, he discovered. Anyway, it must be that I do feel sorry for her; he consoled himself.

After all she's going through a lot right now. Who knows if she's really pregnant. Anyway, after certifying that, on Saturday, I'm sure this sudden fondness will go. He assured himself. He has booked an appointment with a gynaecologist friend of his so Sophie could do a pregnancy test to know if she's really pregnant. What a naïve girl, he thought. She doesn't even seem to know what to do on her own. The mysterious man has not called again. Looks like he got information that he's been recognized or it might even be he's planning another strategy. But then, who else knows about Sophie except Emeka, Angel, Jake, himself and Kings? These are the only people who have all the information connected with the case. He wondered. Maybe they spread it out to other people. He silently concluded with a shrug.

"Do you think we should swear the barrister and his friends to secrecy if they really want progress in this case?" he confided in Kings who agreed with him.

CHAPTER TWELVE

"You aren't pregnant". The doctor announced.

"Are you sure doctor?" Sophie couldn't believe her ears. "I've not seen my period for almost a month now", she reminded him. She had been worrying about how she would give her parents the news, their reaction and the shame that would be associated with it if the result comes out positive. However, Jones has been assuring her that all would be alright and she decided to just trust him. She does not even know what he told her parents about her involvement in the case. "I seem to have so much confidence in that man". She has mused many times.

"According to the test conducted on you, you're not pregnant". The doctor told her showing her the test result. It read negative.

"So what is wrong with me then? Why haven't I seen my normal period? It has never happened like this before". She told the doctor.

"There are a lot of issues responsible for that". He told her, "Like stress, hormonal problem, anxiety, recent surgery etc.

"It must be anxiety then, because I've really gone through a lot in the last few weeks ". She confided.

The doctor, sensing she didn't want to go into details took time to explain to her that prolonged stress, worries, anxiety can affect the normal body function, especially that of women. He advised her to learn to take whatever is worrying her easy, have a lot of rest and with time, all will normalize.

"You mean I'm perfectly okay?" She wanted to be sure.

"Unless you tell me otherwise. If not I don't see anything wrong with you. Just relax and before you know it, your body system will return to normal." He assured her with a smile.

She thanked the doctor and left the office feeling like a heavy burden had been lifted from her shoulders.

"Guess what!" she excitedly asked Jones when she returned to the reception where Jones was patiently waiting for her. He had arrived at their house in the morning to pick her up telling the parents that it was all part of the investigation. They arrived at the hospital apprehensively, but with lots of encouragement from Jones, she had to go ahead with the test and had to wait with bated breath for the final results.

"You don't have to be nervous". Jones had tried to make her relax.

"You don't realize the kind of parents I have and the terrible ordeal I will go through if it's discovered that I'm pregnant." She poured out her fears. "Oh God! What have I foolishly got myself into?" She had wailed.

"Look, getting pregnant isn't the end of the world. Your parents are human beings. It's only natural for them to be upset at first, but with time, they'll have no choice but to accept it. But then, that's if you're really pregnant. He consoled her. She looked at him. "You don't really believe I'm pregnant? What makes you think such? "

"Ehn.., since you don't seem to be having the other pregnancy symptons as you told me, we can only hope it's a false alarm".

"You're so nice and understanding". She told him." But why are you being such to me? You hardly know me". She asked him the question she has been asking herself for sometime recently without finding answers. At first, she had felt it was only natural since she was very important in the investigation as a witness; but then he had gone the extra mile in making arrangements for her to come to this hospital for the test, not to talk of the constant calls to their house to make sure she's ok.

"I really don't know". Jones answered, intruding into her thoughts. "I just know I have a strong urge to protect you. It may be because we're dealing with very dangerous criminals". He explained even though he knows that isn't just the reason. Lately, it has become almost an obsession to see and talk to the girl and he also noticed that he was always very happy and comfortable in her presence. Well, I can't be falling in love with a lady who might be pregnant with another man's child. That would be it. He shook his head helplessly. I've met with a lot of incidents in this my job , he continued silently, but this happens to be a new one, which is completely beyond me. Well, I'll just relax and see what it'll lead to'. He shrugged resignedly. And so, he had waited apprehensively, almost praying for it not to be. Finally, she entered the room. One look at her face, he almost hugged her.

"You aren't pregnant". He correctly whispered, and before they knew it, they were in each others arms in the full glare of other patients. She couldn't care less. A big part of her problems have been solved, and a big thanks to this wonderful man. She didn't think she would have had the courage to do the test herself.

"Really, I don't know how to thank you." She told him after the hug

"You've already done that". He smiled, wondering why he's feeling so happy and relieved. "And that calls for a celebration". He continued. All he knew was that he wanted to spend more time with her.

She was undecided for a time, but on seeing the look on his face, and not wanting to hurt his feelings, she smiled up at him. "You've done a lot for me already. Won't I be taking up so much of your time?" she said.

"No, you won't." He assured her. "Actually I'm enjoying your company". And since she was also enjoying his company, she didn't need a second invitation. "After all, what will I lose?" She asked herself. "I'm not rushing home for anything".

They arrived at 'The crab' in Victoria Island. It was quite a decent restaurant mostly for the upper class. They had settled down when Jones recognized Angel, then Emeka in that order. They were sitting down, two tables away from theirs with Sophie backing them. They appeared so engrossed in themselves that they didn't notice Jones and his partner. "That's Nnamdi's brother". He told Sophie. "Oh!" She replied, turning back to stare in the direction Jones was looking at. "His partner is quite beautiful". She observed.

"Yes, she is. His fiancée". He explained.

"Well, that's quite a consolation, even though she can never replace the brother". "Quite true". Jones agreed. Then turning to the waiter who was patiently waiting for their orders, he ordered drinks and snacks. Soon, they became engrossed with getting to know each other better, that they forgot the couple two tables away. Before long, they found out they had a lot in common. They had the same 'likes' and 'dislikes'. They were still talking when a shadow fell on their table and on looking up, they saw Angel and Emeka standing at their table. They were probably on their way out and, on recognizing Jones, they decided to stop and say 'Hi'.

"Oh! What a nice surprise", Angel smiled at him. Jones stood up to shake hands with them.

"Meet Sophie, the lady who is helping us with the investigation". He introduced them. Both turned to stare at Sophie.

"We're so glad to meet you", Angel began. "We're really grateful for the part you're playing in the investigation. You must come for lunch someday". She invited her.

"Thank you and it's a pleasure meeting you too." Sophie replied, deliberately avoiding the 'Lunch invitation', since she, being the shy and reserved type didn't think she wanted to be involved in the case more than is necessary.

"Any new developments?" Emeka enquired of Jones.

"Nothing for now, but we keep up hope".

"Well, I'm sorry for having been a bit uncooperative , that was as a result of shock. But that's all over now. I want to assure you that I'm in full support of the investigation and also available any time I'm needed." He apologized.

"That's okay. We understand". Jones replies, and shaking hands once again, they departed.

CHAPTER THIRTEEN

Superintedent Okon looked up from his desk to see a young girl of about thirteen years of age, average height and a bit plump standing just by the door of his office. She appeared frightened.

"Come in". he told her.

"Yes, what can I do for you?" He asked when it seemed like she wasn't going to say anything.

"Good morning sir". She greeted.

"Morning, so what's the problem?" he asked, noting that she escaped albinoism by just a quarter.

After a brief hesitation, "I'm looking for Jones, the detective". She replied.

He looked her up and down, wondering what Jones had to do with her.

"Is he expecting you?" He asked.

"No!"

"Why do you want to see her?"

"It's in connection with the murder of Nnamdi'.

He considered her answer. This murder case is developing into something else. He thought. There seems to be no head or tail of the case. The murderers seem to have vanished into thin air. No murder case in their jurisdiction has been as complex as this.

"What's your name?" He asked her.

"Nkoli Eze".

She seemed so nervous and scared. He observed further. Shrugging, he pressed the intercom, seconds later a young man entered and saluted him.

"Is Inspector Jones on sit?" He asked the young man.

"Yes sir".

"Take her to him". He pointed towards Nkoli.

"Nice surprise". Jones exclaimed on seeing Nkoli.

"How do you do, Miss Nkoli?"

He still remembered her name. She silently observed."How do you do sir?" She acknowledged the greeting.

Jones and Kings shared the same office. Their tables face each other, from the opposite sides of the room. The room is large, covered with cream coloured tiles. At one end of the office is an office cabinet with six compartments. Each compartment contains lots of files which had to do with unsolved cases, cases-in-progress or solved cases. The alphabets pasted on each makes it easier to reach a needed file. A large OX fan stood at the other end of the room giving out cool air. At the moment Kings was not around.

"So what does Miss Nkoli need my help for?" He teased, smiling at her in other to make her relax seeing she was uneasy. He had often wondered about her strange behaviour on the first day she was interrogated. But then, he never expected her to turn up so soon.

She still stood, shifting on her legs. He suddenly remembered he hadn't offered her a seat. Quite ungracious of me, he thought.

"Please, do have a seat. Forgive my manners." She thanked him and sat down with a relief.

"I saw the man who killed Nnmadi". She blurted out.

"Wait! Did you say 'man'?" Jones asked.

"Yes". She vigorously nodded. "There's only one man that did it, and I can identify him anywhere". She continued.

Jones stared at her. This is quite a different version, he thought. The case is becoming more complex. Then he brought out his tape recorder.

"Can you tell me exactly what you know?"

She took a deep breath, then started; "On that fateful day, as I was sweeping our own portion of the compound, a red car drove in, on seeing me, the driver slowed down, stopped and beckoned on me. I went over to him. He asked for Nnamdi's house, I showed him innocently because it was quite normal for visitors to the compound to ask for the house of the particular person they were looking for. The man, on getting the needed information from me drove off without even a "Thank you". I could remember saying that he was a rude man. I went back to my work almost immediately. Minutes later, the man drove back and beckoned on me again. I almost didn't go due to his initial reaction, but on second thoughts, I thought he didn't see Nnamdi and probably wanted to give me a message for him, so I went just because of Nnamdi. To my greatest shock and horror, he brought out an evil-looking, sharp knife covered with blood and pointed at me. I couldn't believe my eyes. "If you ever breathe a word about me or this to anybody, I'll deal with you the same way". Those were his exact words. Then before I could recover from my horrified state, he drove away. I was so frightened that I couldn't sweep again. So I ran into the house. Since then, I haven't been at ease, so I finally made up my mind to come and see you when I couldn't bear it again."

Jones, who had been listening intently while she was talking, now wondered where to begin.

"Why didn't you tell me all these on that day?"

"I was scared of the man's threat".

"So, by coming out with it openly , you aren't afraid again?"

"No, like I told you, I've been burdened by it".

He stared at her for some seconds, "Are you in school?" he asked.

"Yes". She answered wondering what it has got to do with the matter at hand.

"Which school?"

"Iyale-Esele Grammar school Mafoluku".

No wonder she speaks good English. It's a good government school. She's lucky to be with such nice guardians. It's a pity she's involved in this case. He thought sadly.

"Can you describe the man in the car?"

She nodded; "He's short, dark and thickset in appearance".

"You said all the time he was talking to you he was inside the car?"

"Yes'.

"How do you know he's short then?"

"I knew, because his head just barely reached the window".

"Can you identify him among a group of other men?"

"Yes, definitely". She eagerly answered. "In fact, I can even picture his face in my mind".

He nodded, looking at her thoughtfully.

"What time of the day did this incident take place?" he asked.

She appeared to be in thought, then finally said it was mid morning, but couldn't remember the exact time.

Mid morning, he thought. Hmmm, it almost coincides with Sophie's time.

"Were you the only person in the compound at that time?"

"At the time, I was."

"Do the people you're living with know about this?"

She shook her head.

"But they have to know because we'll be needing your help from time to time in the investigation."

"No, you don't have to tell them". She hastily objected. "You can just contact me on the phone and I'll make my self available."

"No!" He firmly said wondering which kind of house help has such liberty to come and go as she likes without the consent of her employers. "If you're to help us in this case, the people you're staying with just have to know about it. After all. It wasn't your fault that you were outside at the time the man came".

"I don't think they'll allow me to help". She still insisted.

"Don't worry, I'll talk to them myself." Jones assured her.

She finally gave a resigned shrug and stood up to go.

"Thank you for the information though'. He thanked her.

"You're welcome."

After she left, he sat down and pondered over what she had just told him. It was a completely different story from what sophie gave them. Now the question is: Who is telling the truth among them? But then, in his brief acquaintance with Sophie, she didn't look like someone who would lie about such. But this Nkoli, he hardly knew her. What would she gain by coming here to cook up such a story? Some thing very fishy is definitely going on somewhere. He thought. Anyway, till Kings comes back, then they would both go over the whole story again. Two heads are better than one, they say.

"Darling, I'm so happy you're back to your normal self". Angel said.

They were in Emeka's house and she was relaxing in his arms.

"All thanks to you my love. I don't know how I would have managed without your love and care. In fact, immediately this murder case is resolved, we'll set our wedding date."

She was silent for a while.

"What's wrong dear? Don't you want to marry me again?" He looked worried.

"No, it's not that." She smiled and gave him a kiss. Of course, there's no other man I would like to spend the rest of my life with". She assured him. "It's just that I'm wondering how long we'll have to wait to get married, judging from what you said. What if the murderers are never discovered, does it mean we'll wait forever? He smiled, relieved.

"I understand what you mean. I'm as eager for us to be together forever but then, you have to remember that the murdered man is my own flesh and blood, and my only sibling in this world. We have to accord him that respect, unless the detectives decide to give up. " he explained. "God save those murderers if found". He angrily shook his head slowly.

"What will you do to them? She asked, frightened by the look on his face.

"Till they're discovered." He seemed far away.

Angel suddenly sat up and ran her fingers up and down his cheek in a bid to lighten his sudden change of mood.

"Darling, I know how you must feel. It's a natural feeling but you don't have to overdo it. You might end up putting yourself into trouble. Remember, to err is human; to forgive, divine. You must forgive them." She desperately pleaded.

Emeka stared at her. "Are you trying to tell me that murdering my own brother is an error?" he couldn't believe his ears.

She was about to defend herself when Emeka's phone rang. It was Jones who after the usual pleasantries told him about Nkoli's story.

"So, what we you going to do?" Emeka asked him.

"It's a bit complicated but nothing is beyond being solved. We'll surely get to the root of the matter." He assured Emeka. "We just felt you should be kept current with whatever is happening."

"I appreciate that and good luck".

"Yeah, thanks. We need that." They dropped.

He told Angel about the conversation with Jones.

"It's getting complex." She observed, and Emeka nodded.

"Emy", Angel began after some moments. "I'll be travelling to the east for a burial."

"When?"

"Most probably tomorrow."

"So soon...? Whose?"

"A friend's dad."

"How long will you stay?"

"I can't really say now. It depends on how long my friend will need me."

He took her in his arms. "Darling, you always carry people's problems as if they're yours. I'm sorry for snapping at you moments ago. I was worked up. The thought of these murderers brings out the worst in me." He apologized.

"I understand." She smiled, patting his cheeks.

"I love you." He assured her.

"Same here". She replied back.

CHAPTER FOURTEEN

ATTAMCO Nig Ltd, boldly written in black letters on an orange rectangular plate indicates the company they were looking for. The gateman opened the large black gate after finding out their identity through a Judas window built into the gate. The compound was very large, with many bungalows serving as offices arranged in double rows; each facing each other. They were about eight rows. The security called someone to lead them to Mr Schechem's office. A young lady of about twenty nine years sat behind a table with a desk top computer in front of her which she was operating. She wore a pair of thick spectacles, giving her a serious appearance. Her hair was tightly tied back with a large grey-coloured hair band, making her look severe. She looked up briefly from her work, took in the two men at a glance, then went back to work.

Jones cleared his throat. "Good day young lady." He greeted.

"Good day." She answered without looking up.

"We're looking for Mr Schechem." He told her when it seemed like they were going to stand there forever.

"He's not in." She replied, still busy with her work.

Kings suddenly stepped forward and shoved his I.D right under her nose. She was about to glare at him when her eyes caught the words on the car. Her demeanor changed immediately. She seemed to suddenly loose her composure. She looked up immediately.

"Is he in or not?" Jones barked in his cop voice.

"I'm telling the truth. He left this morning, shortly after he arrived at the office, on a business trip. He's expected back tomorrow." She hastily explained.

Jones and Kings exchanged glances.

"We'll be back next tomorrow. I hope he'll be in by then." Jones said.

"Sure, he will." She promised.

They turned and left. "Looks like luck's not on our side today." Jones said as they left the office. Kings suggested they look round the company. As they went round, Jones asked his partner what he thought of Nkoli's story. He had replayed the story for Kings when he came back to the office long after Nkoli had gone. After listening, Kings said he would like to think about it before they decide what to do next.

"It doesn't really have substance in it and seems made up, I think." Kings answered.

" That's what I thought as well, yet one can't understand why the girl decided to take such an action." Jones wondered, but a bit relieved that he and Kings agreed on one thing in this case.

"Well, I think we just have to play along with her till she solves the mystery herself. Meanwhile, I suggest we keep everything we're doing or hearing now a secret, not even Emeka and his friends should know anything because this is getting complicated. Right now, nobody should be trusted. Not even Sophie." He glanced at Jones.

Jones agreed even though he felt that Emeka should at least be kept updated, but then Kings has always been right judging by previous investigations." He remembered.

    Sophie was about to enter her bedroom for a short rest after lunch when the land phone in their sitting room rang. She heard her mum pick it, and then after a while, shouted up to her that Jones wanted to speak with her. Her heart beating wildly, she ran downstairs, nearly knocking down her sister who was coming upstairs. Olivia smiled knowingly. After their visit to the doctor, Sophie hadn't heard from Jones again. That was when she realized that she was getting fond of him. She had been itching to see or hear from him again and had been wondering why he hadn't called , especially as he used to come or call almost everyday before the visit to the doctor. She hadn't dared to contact him first because she didn't have anything useful to tell him. She had tried so hard to remove him from her mind, yet she couldn't. I can't seem to stop myself from liking him, she thought. Oh God! She had cried for the umpteenth time. I'm in for another heart break. This one won't even look at me as anything except an instrument for unraveling a murder case after which I'll be forgotten. Poor me! She had cried so many times. She tried to control herself when she reached downstairs and saw her mum looking at her strangely as she held out the phone. Well, who cares? She thought and took the phone from her.

"Hello." She said into the mouthpiece, trying very hard to steady her voice and hands which were shaking much to her annoyance.

"So, how is my premature pregnant friend doing?" Jones teased.

She laughed. She always felt comfortable and happy in his company. He has a way of making people feel at ease with him.

"Well, she is still recovering from the premature birth." She equally matched his teasing tone.

He laughed. "I'm sorry I haven't contacted you in a long time." He apologized. In fact, he had to exercise self control to have achieved that, since he noticed that he was falling in love with the lady and that would be dangerous. He definitely can't do anything about it until the murderers are brought to book. Moreover he isn't even sure of her feelings towards him. She also seemed happy and relaxed in his company but then she had to be, he was helping her so she had to appear grateful. He didn't think she would be in a hurry to enter another relationship so soon, after the trauma of the first. But then, man proposes, God disposes; as the saying goes. Angel had called him early that morning, inviting him and Sophie for lunch. He promised to contact Sophie and that all depended on her. She then told him to persuade her since she couldn't think of any other way of thanking her for her help in the investigation. They would really love to have her as a guest in their house. She implored. Jones promised to do all he could.

" I've been wondering what I did to offend you." Sophie intruded into his thoughts.

"No dear," he laughed. He always laughs in her company. "Actually, the whole case is getting more complicated so I hardly have time to myself nowadays."

"Anyway, I do understand. Just take it easy." She advised .

"I will." He agreed. "How about lunch at Barrister Emeka Ngene's house, Nnamdi's brother?"

Sophie stiffened. "Is the offer on already?" She wondered. "I don't understand." She said.

"Well, I got a call from Angel, his fiancée inviting you and I to lunch at their house. You remember she mentioned it when we met at 'The Crab'. He reminded her.

"I remember, but I didn't think it would be so soon." Actually she didn't feel like going. She didn't know why, but the thought of going there at all gave her goose pimples and made her ill at ease.

"So...?" Jones waited

"Eh...n", She cleared her throat. "I don't know why she's eager to have lunch with me. I mean, I don't understand. She owes me nothing".

"I think she just wants to be friendly. Come on, she's only being nice. It wouldn't do you any harm. After all, I'll be there as well." He assured her.

"Okay! I accept". She half heartedly agreed after a pause.

That's my girl. I'll be there at one pm tomorrow." He promised. Well, at least, I'll have an opportunity to see and be with him again. She consoled herself as she was not even excited about the lunch invitation.

At exactly ten o'clock the next day, Jones was at ATTAMCO Nig Ltd. One glance at him, the secretary rushed in to inform the manager about him. He was ushered in. Mr Schechem's office was large, well covered with white and brown ceramic tiles. On one side of the wall was a large three-seater leather armchair. The man sitting behind a long and wide glass table was a white. He looked too young to be a manager, seemed to be around thirty four years old. His straw coloured hair was thick and neat. His rather fleshy but distinctly handsome face was heavily sun burned. He probably spends a lot of time under the sun. his pointed nose was rather small when compared to his pair of large eyes. His lips were red making it look like he had on red lipstick, and thin. The office was cool with the air conditioner on, and comfortable.

After the usual greeting, the man waved him to a chair and he took the one directly opposite him so he could observe him very well while he talked. Somehow, he was happy Mr Schechem is a white man as they're usually more cooperative and straightforward than the blacks based on his previous experiences in the job. He produced his ID card, introducing himself.

"Yes, my secretary told me about you. How can I be of help?" Schechem asked.

"I'm investigating the murder of a young man, Engr Nnamdi Ngene." He said, looking at the man for any sign of recognition. The man's face suddenly brightened, then turned sad almost immediately. Sadly, he shook his head. "His death is a terrible blow to the company." He said solemnly.

Jones stared at him flabbergasted. What is the man talking about? He wondered. Is this where Nnamdi worked? Suddenly the name, 'ATTAMCO' clicked. That's where Sophie said Nnamdi worked. Strange it escaped he and Kings' minds, or did it escape Kings'? he wondered, recalling how he had suggested that they walked round the compound that day. He could remember not having seen the reason for that as they finally left without finding anything unusual. This is getting interesting. He smiled inwardly.

"You mean he was a member of staff here?" He wanted a further confirmation. Mr Schechem stared at him as if he was out of his mind.

"Then why did you decide to come here at all if you didn't know he was a staff?" he asked suspiciously.

"Just routine question". Jones calmed him. "Can you tell me anything about Nnamdi that would help in the investigation?" He continued.

The man looked up thoughtfully for a while. "I think his colleagues in his department will be in a better position to help you". All I can tell you is that he was one of our best engineers; very hardworking, knew what he wanted. In fact, he just won a huge contract which would have attracted a huge sum of money. Whoever murdered him must be nuts." He finished sadly.

"Which department was he in?"

"Productions."

"This is ......?" he waved round the office.

"Administrations."

"You mean you were hardly in personal contact with him then?"

"I wouldn't say, 'hardly', because he often used to come here to discuss certain issues which required my help. Actually, I was the one who helped him in securing the contract which as a matter of fact was really meant for his partner, but due to the fact that he was smarter, he got it instead. That's number one positive factor in business, 'Smartness'.

"Do you think the aggrieved partner might have a hand in his death since he has enough reasons to harbor ill feelings towards him?"

Mr Schechem shook his head. "Actually, that's the normal thing to think, but when you see the man in question, you will have no choice but to dispel the notion from your mind. He looks completely harmless. I also heard both of them were very close, almost like brothers such that the death so devastated him that for some days, he was a shadow of himself."

"Is it possible for me to see the man?"

"Most certainly, that's why I referred you to Engr Ngene's department originally. The man's name is Mr Keneka."

"Do you by any chance know a Mr Jake?" Jones continued.

"No, I don't." He answered after a short pause in which he appeared to be thinking.

"He mentioned you as his friend through whom he got to know of the murdered man."

He shook his head slowly, "I don't know him, except he goes by another name".

"Ok, thank you for your time." He told Schechem who shook hands with him and promised to help in anyway he could.

Outside the office, the secretary helped in directing him to productions department. Just as he was about to leave her office for the department based on her description, a man came into the secretary's office. She then told Jones that the man was working at the productions and could help him. On enquiry, he found out from the man that Mr Keneka just left the office less than ten minutes ago but promised to be back soon. However, he decided to be back the next day as he had other engagements and therefore couldn't wait.

Jones was on his way back to his office after his visit to ATTAMCO when Sophie suddenly popped into his head. The girl hadn't been so comfortable during the lunch at Emeka's house the previous day. At first, he thought she was just being shy, but Angel and Emeka had been the perfect hosts and the food was superb. He had to give Angel the extra credit. She was an excellent cook. The lady seems perfect in everything. Really, she was too good to be true. Emeka is a lucky man, he envied him. They had both gone out of their way to make him and Sophie comfortable yet he knew Sophie wasn't at ease. He didn't know whether others noticed it, but he almost knew her very well now, at least to know when she's okay and when she isn't, and in this particular instance, she wasn't. He noticed that she had kept stealing glances at Angel when she wasn't looking. It seemed as if she was trying to remember something, yet she couldn't.

On their way back from Emeka's house, he had had to ask her what was wrong, she only replied that she couldn't pin point exactly what it was but she knew something wasn't exactly right. She had actually tried her best there, she confirmed but she had a premonition that something was wrong somewhere. She felt bad because she had destroyed what would've been a very nice outing, most especially as she was with the one person who makes her happy lately. Jones on his part, felt sorry for the agony she was going through even though he couldn't understand it. He felt she was still suffering from the shock of the murder. With time, she'll get over it. He consoled himself. He had dropped her with a promise of calling more often, also reminding her to call him should any strange thing happen.

He had told Kings all about his visit to ATTAMCO even though he hadn't had much to say about it. Anyway, his partner had never really been a man of many words. He believed in action instead. He had only suggested they go back again two days later instead of the next day as promised for reasons best known to him. On the evening of that same day, Kings paid Emeka visit. Jones had told him about the lunch at the Barrister's house. He was warmly received by Emeka, and on enquiry was told that Angel travelled the previous day.

"It must have been after the lunch". It was more of a statement than a question.

"Yes", Emeka answered. "She took the night flight".

Not a man of many words, Kings went on to tell him the latest development in the matter which includes the discovery that Jake wasn't known to Mr Schechem unless by another name. Emeka confirmed that it had to be the later suggestion.

"Jake is too loyal. He's really a friend in need and so couldn't have been lying."

"So, what's his surname?" Kings asked. They had omitted getting his full name when he was questioned. Emeka tried to see if he could recall Jake's surname but couldn't. "It's been such a long time, he thought. He remembered Jake because that was his popular name at school. His surname wasn't commonly used then.

"I'm sorry, it's been very long. I can't remember." He apologized to Kings.

"What of his residential address?" Kings couldn't imagine why they omitted the vital questions.

Once again, Emeka shook his head sadly. He and Angel seemed to have taken Jake's friendship for granted. They never bothered to go and visit him. It seemed Jake had been the one doing all the visits and calls. He was filled with remorse.

"What of his office address?"

"This is really embarrassing. Which kind of friend am I?" He said aloud after shaking his head.

Kings stood up. "I'll keep in touch. My regards to your fiancée". He extended his hand for a handshake.

"It's too bad I was of little help, but don't worry. Jake calls often. Once he does, I'll get the required information from him." He promised.

Kings nodded, requested of him not to let Jones know about his visit, telling him it's all part of the investigation. Then he left.

Emeka was still pondering over Kings' visit when the phone rang, it was Angel.

"Darling, I miss you so much. How're you?"

"I'm good. Miss you too. How is the burial going?"

'Good!".

He then went into a detailed account of what took place between him and Kings.

"Well, we can do nothing but keep our fingers crossed. They are professionals you know and therefore know how to do their jobs. I wish I'm there with you anyway."

"It's okay dear, I'm handling it well."

"Somehow I don't think everything is alright. Does it mean the Sophie girl is lying then?"

"That's what nobody can fathom. It might be any of them. Sophie's story has more substance it seems, than Nkoli's. Anyway, don't bother yourself about it. Just concentrate on what you travelled for. Hopefully, by the time you come back, the mystery must have been solved. Ok?" he assured her.

After a little silence in which she seemed to be thinking about what he said,

"Have you heard from Jake?" She enquired.

He answered in the negative and went further to tell her about the detective's story on Jake, and the fact that they hardly knew anything about him.

"Do you think Jake is an impostor then?" She asked, sounding worried.

Emeka laughed, assuring her of Jake's sincerity. "I've known him since Secondary school you know. Never knew him to be a criminal. So don't worry, as far as I'm concerned, he's clean." He defended Jake.

"Ok, if you say so. You'll have to find out all the necessary information from him then when next he calls. It's quite thoughtless of us not to have bothered finding out anything about him."

"That's right." Emeka concurred.

After a few more exchange of affectionate words between them, they ended the call.

Two days after Jones visit to ATTAMCO, he and Kings paid another visit to the company. The place looked more lively than it was on their previous visit. On enquiry, they were led to the productions unit. The building, though similar to that of the administrative section was different inside. On entering the building, one was almost deafened by a noise seeming as if something was being ground, yet one couldn't pinpoint where the noise was coming from since all the doors on either side of the long corridor were closed. After some hesitation, Jones knocked on the door directly opposite the main entrance since nobody was in sight to be asked for Keneka's office. Since there was no response to his knock, he tried the door handle which gave way and he and Kings found themselves starring into a simply furnished but comfortable looking office. The room contained three tables arranged in a semi-circle all facing the door. Behind each table was a brown leather armchair. On one side of the wall, a three seater executive chair was placed. The floor was covered with grey ceramic tiles. The office was fully air conditioned, judging by the cool air which hit them instantly on entry, compared with the hot one on the outside. Both men took in all these at a glance. A young lady who seemed to be the only occupant of the room was standing near a large cupboard in the room, probably about to open it when the men entered. She signaled them to close the door which was as well because she would've had to scream to be heard above the defeaning noise. They complied and there was a sudden silence in the room.

"The walls are sound proof" The lady explained due to the look of astonishment on their faces. She must have been used to doing that to visitors since she did it matter of factly as if it was an everyday occurrence.

"For a moment, I thought we were in a war zone." Jones joked.

The lady laughed. "This is productions so the noise is normal. The factory is in this building. However, the noise is only heard in the corridor as all the offices here are sound proof."

"Please do sit down." She offered, indicating the three-seater executive chair.

"I'm afraid I'm the only person in the office right now."

They both sat down and Jones used the opportunity to closely observe the lady. She was about twenty six years, fair in complexion, tall and slender. She had a charming, though not so beautiful face, seemed friendly and well mannered from the way she received them.

"Ehn..". Jones cleared his throat. "We're looking for Mr Keneka's office." He started.

"This is his office, but he's not on seat right now." She answered.

He looked at his watch. It was a quarter to ten o'clock."

"He went out or he hasn't come?" he asked.

"No", she shook her head. "You don't understand. He's on leave." She explained.

"I was here two days ago, no one talked of him being on leave." Jones was surprised.

"He just requested for it yesterday, and the management agreed almost immediately, probably because of his condition."

"Which condition?"

"We lost one of our colleagues and they were quite close. His death had been affecting Keneka."

"Are you his relatives?" She asked after a pause, seeing how Jones face became clouded on hearing that Keneka was on leave.

Jones felt it was time to introduce themselves so they brought out their ID card and introduced themselves and their mission.

"Oh! Detectives." She muttered. "That's Nnamdi's table". She pointed to the one at the extreme left side of the room. "He was such a dear and jolly fellow." She soliloquized. "As a matter of fact, since his death, this office has lost most of its shine. It was never this dull and quiet when he was alive."

"What was his relationship with Keneka like?"

"They were very close, like brothers. It's going to take Keneka quite some time to recover from the shock. That's mainly the reason why he took that leave."

"But don't you think he took that leave a bit late; Nnamdi didn't just die two days ago." Kings asked for the first time.

"Well, I really don't know. Probably he thought he would cope at first, but later discovered he couldn't. Everything in this office reminds him of Nnamdi." She offered.

"What of you, were you not close to Nnamdi?" Kings continued.

She looked at him as if he had spoken a foreign language.

"Who was not close to Nnamdi? We were like a family, the three of us. But then, I wasn't as close to him as Keneka was. You know, birds of the same feathers flock together. They were both males and I, female if you understand. However,

I was terribly affected though not to the extent of having to leave the office on leave. She explained.

"I understand he got the contract originally meant for Keneka." Jones asked.

"Yes, he did."

"So, how did it affect their relationship since you're the closest to them in the office."

"I told you they were like brothers. Keneka was even the first to congratulate him, and told him the dividend must be shared fifty-fifty jokingly." Sometimes, he even used to tell Nnamdi that he took pity on him and left the contract for him in order to alleviate his poor status. He was not jealous at all and it didn't affect their friendship."

"So, you don't think he would have anything to do with Nnamdi's death?"

Shaking her head vehemently, she answered in the negative. "Not Keneka. He can't even hurt a fly. You need to see him."

"Was Nnamdi on bad terms with anybody in this company?"

"None that I know of. Nnamdi was everybody's friend, but then if there was anyone that had any grievance against him, I don't know. But ever since I got to know him, I never for once heard him complain or say any bad thing about anyone. He would always make excuses for people's bad behaviour. Whoever murdered him must truly be a nutcase." She vehemently said.

"So how can we meet Keneka? Can you give us his residential address? Phone no?"

"He wouldn't be in his house, though I don't have it, but he told me he would be travelling outside Lagos that yesterday. I can give you his phone no." She offered.

"It's quite strange that as close as you are in this office, you don't have each other's residential addresses." Jones was surprised.

"Ah... I know Nnamdi's. Infact, it's impossible not to know his." She defended.

"Impossible.... how?"

"He almost used to sing it as a song. 'If you need me anytime, just call at N0 20 Lakunle street, Ajao; I'm always available.' He had nothing to hide."

"But Keneka had?" Kings asked.

She hesitated before replying that. "I didn't exactly mean that. Different strokes for different folks you know. While Nnamdi was an extrovert, Keneka is an introvert." She hastily explained.

"Is Keneka the first name or the surname?" Jones asked.

"I've always known him as Mr keneka."

"Who is his other close friend in this office?"

"None that I know of. He doesn't have many friends."

"Ok, can we have the phone no please?"

She hesitated a while. "He's really going to be pissed with me for giving his number without his consent."

"No problem. You can call him first and seek his consent." Kings told her.

She dialed his no, but it wasn't going through. After a series of dials and not getting through. "Looks like he switched off his phone." She told them.

"Well, you can send him a message explaining what you had to do and the effort you made to get his consent."

She did that and gave them his number. They thanked her for her co-operation and left.

"It still looks like a dead end." Jones put his thoughts into words as they drove out of the compound. When Kings offered no reply, Jones stole a glance at him and noticed that he seemed deep in thought.

"Has anyone of Nkoli's description been found?" he asked Jones.

"Yes, but none has been identified by her." Nkoli has been called twice to identify her man, but none has been successful.

"I have a strong conviction that story was made up but I don't want to conclude yet." Kings volunteered.

"Same here." Jones agreed.

The rest of the ride was done in silence. Each man absorbed in his own thoughts.

CHAPTER FIFTEEN

A week later, Kings phoned Emeka and learnt that Angel was back. "She just came back yesterday, but she's down with fever. Though she attributed it to stress, I'm still worried about her especially as she wouldn't agree to visit the hospital." Emeka complained. He had tried to persuade her to allow them see a doctor that morning when she was too weak to get up from the bed, but she had refused, saying he was over reacting and that she only needed a little rest since she over stressed herself at the burial. Emeka agreed, but is still a bit worried. So when Kings called, he was just glad to confide in somebody. "Okay, don't worry." Kings assured him. "I'll just get a doctor of mine to examine her. In that case, she wouldn't need to go to the hospital."

"I'll really appreciate that."Emeka thanked him.

"What of Jake, have you heard from him?"

"No, in fact, I'm worried about him. He used to call almost daily, but since the last time you visited, he hasn't called, and his phone seems constantly switched off."

Kings said nothing to that, promised he was on his way and dropped the phone.

Nkoli was almost on her way to the market when Kings and Jones stopped in front of their house. At first, she thought she was needed at the station for more identification, but they asked for Onyeka. The young doctor was relaxing with his sister in the sitting room watching the television. After the usual exchange of pleasantries, Kings explained that he would like Onyeka to accompany him to look at a sick friend.

"Why me?" Onyeka was surprised. "I mean, there are many more experienced and qualified medical doctors around." He informed them.

"Obviously...." Kings acquiesced. "But right now, none is willing to leave his hospital and follow me to a friend's house. C'mon, the person is running a temperature. Aren't you a medical doctor too, even if you just graduated? You've got to start from somewhere." Kings persuaded him.

Emeka opened the door for them. As Onyeka was being introduced, Angel came into the sitting room. She really looked sick though it didn't lessen her obvious beauty.

"That's the lady that came looking for Nnamdi with another lady." Onyeka blurted out before he could help himself. He stood up. He couldn't believe his eyes. What a coincidence. He never thought he would see that face again. He turned to stare at Kings, Jones, Emeka, then back to Angel. Everyone looked confused except Kings who looked on calmly and actually seemed to be enjoying the scene unfolding.

"But you said the lady had a beauty spot." Jones asked, not exactly understanding what was going on.

"I'm very positive about this. This is the taller and prettier lady. I will recognize that face anywhere, anytime. It's not common." He insisted. "Were you not the lady who came with another, asking for 'Brother Nnamdi' at my compound?" he asked her. Angel stared at him looking completely bewildered.

"Are you suggesting that my wife has a hand in my brother's death?" Emeka couldn't believe what he was seeing and hearing. He was ready to throw Onyeka out of his house. "Who is this mad man you brought to my house to accuse and insult my wife?" he asked. "Imagine, when did my wife start moving around with Bible looking for 'brothers and sisters'?" he was livid with anger. Onyeka couldn't take it anymore. Turning on his heels, he marched out of the house. Kings signaled Jones to follow him while he went towards Angel who had sat down suddenly after the first shock. Bending down towards her to apologise for what happened, his pocket note book fell out of his shirt pocket onto Angel's lap. She immediately picked it up and gave hm. He thanked her, took it from her, holding it with just his thumb and fore finger.

"I'm really sorry for what happened just now." He apologized. "I was only trying to help out."

"It's okay." Emeka accepted the apology. "I think we'll just like to be alone now, please." He politely told Kings desperately wanting to explain everything to his fiancée who was still looking confused.

"Sure." Kings agreed. "We'll keep in touch." And he left.

Meanwhile, Jones had caught up with Onyeka who was in such a hurry to leave that place. "That's the lady. I'm very sure of that. Those eyes..., how can I forget them? I kept staring at them while we were talking." He turned to Jones. "What's the meaning of all these? Why was I brought here? Who is the sick person?" Jones was as blank as he.

"Are you sure she's the same person?" Jones finally found his voice. "Do you realize the gravity of what you're saying? People do look alike you know."

"What are you saying?" Onyeka angrily turned to him. "Do you think I talk anyhow? Meanwhile, where's that small man?" He was referring to Kings. "I can't stay here anymore." He continued.

At that moment, Kings appeared apologizing profusely to Onyeka for the insult he received from Emeka, but seemed inwardly pleased and very calm. Jones felt as if the world was going mad. What is Kings up to? He wondered. When they dropped Onyeka, Jones couldn't contol himself anymore. "What are you up to?" He asked Kings.

"What do you mean?" Kings feigned innocence.

"You know very well what I'm talking about."

Kings sighed resignedly and assured him that he thinks they're on their way to unraveling the whole murder mystery but that Jones should exercise a little patience for him to complete the plan he has in mind.

"Have you seen Sophie recently?" he asked Jones.

Jones, a bit surprised by the sudden question, answered in the negative. The last time he saw her was the day they had that lunch. He hadn't even called her. He was positively avoiding her because he has now realized that he is deeply in love with her and he doesn't want to enter a relationship right now, especially with her, a witness in the case, while it's still on.

"Why do you ask?" he asked Kings.

"Just curiosity."

"Are you alright darling?" Emeka asked Angel moving towards her to gather her in his arms. She was still looking pale, apparently not having recovered from the unfortunate drama which just occurred.

"Who was that?" she asked.

Emeka explained about how he had complained to Kings about her condition and how he had offered to help by bringing along a doctor friend. She turned to stare at him. "But I told you I didn't need a doctor, that I was only suffering from stress and just needed a rest." She reminded him.

"I know. I was just worried." He defended himself.

"It's okay." She tenderly touched his cheek. "I think I'll have to go to my parents for a while, at least to get my wind back because this investigation might not really give me as much rest as I need if I stay on here." She suggested to him.

Emeka thought for a while but finally agree since he didn't want a repeat performance of what happened before to occur again.

"I'll drop you." He offered when she was ready, deciding to use the opportunity to meet her parents formally. Since the night he dropped her off, he hadn't been to her place again. She was always almost at his place, preferring to go to the parents after he has left for work. Her reason is always that the parents are so strict and wouldn't hear about relationship with the opposite sex except if it's for marriage. Today, he was determined to take the bull by the horn by getting to know the place well, meeting them and stating his intentions.

They reached her house, but when Emeka offered to come in, she discouraged him saying that she had to prepare her parents first before he could meet them. He reluctantly agreed even though he thought that by now, their relationship isn't supposed to be a secret anymore between members of both families. However, he didn't want to put her into trouble so he drove off after waving at her.

Kings called the next day and after apologizing again for the previous day's incident, asked after Angel and was told that she went to her parents house that same day for a proper rest since they didn't allow her to have it in his house. He also found out that nothing had been heard from Jake. "I'm worried about him." Emeka confided, but then he didn't know where to look for or who to ask for him.

That same evening, Jones and Kings arrived at 17 Jumota street, Ikeja. Kings told Jones they were going to Angel's house to see how she was faring and to enable them properly apologise for yesterday's incident. The house was a three storey building in a less dense area of Ikeja. On enquiry, Angel's house was found on the first floor. Kings asked specifically for her house. Jones pressed the bell and a young lady of about thirty years slightly opened the door after a few minutes. Both observed her. She was on the average side, dark in complexion and slender, but there was no resemblance between her and Angel.

"Is this Dakar's house?" Jones asked.

The lady looked blank for a while, then suddenly brightened up as if something just occurred to her. "Oh! Yes." She answered, "But they're not in right now."

"Actually, it's their daughter Angel we came for. Can we see her?" Kings asked

"Who are you?" The lady requested.

Jones brought out his ID feeling it was time for action. "Now, will you let us in?" He barked.

The lady didn't even budge. Guessing that Jones might resort to force, Kings quickly came in. "So where did she go to then since you don't want to let us in?" he asked in a gentle voice even though the lady never said she wasn't in. She was thrown off balance by the gentility since she was already prepared for trouble.

She stammered the first thing that entered her head. "She ….she went to her boyfriend's place. But I'm expecting her back today." She quickly added on realizing that she probably said the wrong thing. '

"So, what's your relationship with her?" kings asked, regarding her thoughtfully."

"I'm just a relative staying with them."

"What of the parents, when are they expected back?" Kings continued.

"They travelled and won't be back soon."

Seeing it was no use trying to enter the house except by force which Kings felt it wasn't wise to use, they decided to leave, promising to call back later in the day. "Do we try Emeka's house then?" Jones was worried. "That lady didn't seem like she was telling the truth. I think she's hiding something. I just hope Angel is safe. "Don't worry, she's very safe. We'll just wait for her here." Kings told him. They entered their car and drove off from the compound as if they were leaving. At the end of the street, they entered the opposite street, reversed and slowly came back to the street. They parked at a hidden corner of the street, keeping Angel's compound in view. Then they started to wait. Jones being the driver just obeyed every instruction silently, knowing that in the long run, he'll surely get all the gist. Experience has thought him that when Kings is in this mood, it was best not to disturb him with any questions but just to obey as he has always ended up right.

  Twenty minutes after they parked, two ladies came out of the compound. One was tall and slender. She was wearing a gold coloured wig and a pair of dark shades. Her partner was also slender but shorter. On closer look, they recognized her as the lady they had just spoken to. The two ladies were both putting on large t-shirts tucked into tight pair of black jeans. Jones wondered where he had seen the gold wig and dark shades before.

"The lady with the shades looks familiar." He observed. Kings agreed but didn't say a word. The two ladies looked left and right but didn't notice the car containing the two men. They both seemed nervous. Kings looked at his watch; it was a quarter past seven pm. After standing for about three minutes, they flagged down a taxi. Kings quickly motioned Jones to cautiously follow the taxi. Jones quickly obeyed. He was getting excited now even though he didn't know what was happening. The taxi stopped in front of blue gate hotel. Jones moved on a little further so as not to arouse the ladies interest. Kings observed them from his side mirror. The ladies came out of the car, glanced without interest at the car parked a few metres from where they were standing. Then they casually entered the hotel. The detective gave them ten minutes, then Jones reversed according to Kings' orders and drove into the hotel premises, parked and they jumped out of the car. The compound was well lit with large flash bulbs exposing the beauty of the place. The plush interior of the hotel was luxury itself. A few people were relaxing at one end of the wide beautifully furnished hall watching a game of football on the giant sized LED television on the wall. They were very absorbed. The two ladies were not among the group. They looked around, but the other tables were quite empty except for a couple apparently having dinner. They moved towards the reception where a young man, most probably the receptionist gave them a bored look and stifled a yawn as they approached. Apparently they didn't look like the nouveau rich who frequented the hotel. He was casually dressed in a light blue shirt and a pair of dark blue trouser.

"Yes?" He asked when they reached him. Kings brought out his ID and shoved it under his nose. In a hard cop voice he demanded to know the room both ladies checked into. The young man quickly lost his bored look and insulting tone and an expression of fear entered his eyes.

"The police!" he exclaimed. "Please we don't want trouble here." He pleaded.

"That would be if you co-operate with us." Kings assured him.

"Eh...n". He hesitated.

"Which room?" Kings barked. With shaky hands, the boy opened the large book in front of him and quickly glanced through, then raised his head.

"Room 804." He offered.

"How do we find it?" He pointed towards an open door on his right, leading to a stair case.

"Upstairs." He said.

They advised him that in other to avoid trouble he should keep his mouth shut. He nodded and they walked towards the open door which led to a wide corridor. They climbed up the staircase to face two rows of doors facing one another. The odd numbers were on the left while the even numbers were on the right. In that order, they located room 804. Kings told Jones to step aside and told him what to do. Jones obeyed. Kings knocked on the door. At first, there was silence, then a lady's voice asked who it was.

"Room service." Kings answered, then quickly pushed into the room when the door was opened. Jake was reclining on the bed wearing only a pair of black trousers. Angel had removed the wig and dark shades and was sitting on the large settee in the room. She half stood up when kings entered. The other lady who opened the door was still standing and staring at Kings, she then turned to Angel, to Jake and back to Kings. Before any of them could act, Kings pulled out the key from the door and gave Jones who was still outside, then banged the door for Jones to lock making it impossible to leave the room.

"The gang at last". Kings cheerfully broke the silence. "Mr Keneka". He addressed Jake. How do you do? I can see you're really enjoying your leave." he continued sarcastically.

"What's he doing here?" Jake finally found his voice, addressing no one in particular.

"How would I know?" Angel shouted. "I've always known this man is dangerous." She glared at Kings with all the hatred in her being.

"Not as dangerous as you, the faultless fiancé." Kings answered back smiling. "I thought you weren't well. I wonder what your dear boyfriend who is worried about the health of his dear fiancée would say." Angel could have cheerfully killed him with her eyes if they were capable of performing such an act. Suddenly an idea entered her head.

"What can you do then? You can't prove anything, you ingrate." She screamed, then turning to Jake and the other lady; "We can finish him up as well and disappear.

Nobody will know. After all he's here alone." She suggested.

"Do you imagine this smart man would take the risk of coming here alone?" Jake asked her, not moving an inch from where he was sitting. "There's nothing we can do again, it's all over. " He admittedly resignedly.

"What do you mean by 'It's all over'?" Angel shouted. "Are you giving up so easily? C'mon." She persuaded them while kings looked on calmly, sure that everything being said was being recorded.

"What do we do then?" Jake asked. "There's no weapon in this room."

"It's easy. We strangle him. Nobody can prove anything. We can always lie our way out, after all, he's the only difficult one among the two. The other one can be easily convinced." Angel was desperate.

"Okay!" Jake stood up. "Quite an idea. Let's go for it then." He started moving towards Kings.

"You'll only be doubling your crime." Kings calmly told them.

"Don't listen to him, he's only trying to delay us. " Angel shouted, highly agitated now. Move it!" She commanded.

Jake jumped on Kings and in the ensuing struggle between them, Angel motioned to the other lady who had been rooted to a spot since the whole drama, to join in pushing Kings towards the bed. They finally succeeded, Angel held his hands firmly over his head, the other lady stuffed his mouth with a piece of cloth, Jake picked up the pillow, placed it on his neck and was about to press down with all his might when the door burst open revealing half a dozen policemen all pointing their guns at the small party on the bed. "Hold it!" Jones shouted, on seeing what was about to happen. Jake's hands were suspended in mid-air. Angel released Kings and looked around wildly for an escape route but it was impossible. Jones couldn't believe what he was seeing. What is Angel doing here? He wondered, and why is she looking so harassed? The other lady screamed. Kings pushed off Jake and sat up calmly removing the cloth from his mouth.

"Thanks for arriving just in time. I was about to say my last prayers." He smiled at Jones and the police men. Standing up; "I present the murderers of Engr

Nnamdi Ngene." He said, waving his hands towards the trio.

Jones swung into action, "What are you still waiting for?" he barked at the police men. Arrest them!" He commanded. The cops rushed to do his bidding.

"We still have one of them at No. 2 Lakunle street, Ajao Estate; Nkoli by name." Kings informed them. Angel shot him a murderous look as she was handcuffed. Kings smiled cheerfully back at her. Just at that moment, Jones phone started ringing. It was Sophie.

"I have finally remembered where I've seen Angel before." She said. "You won't believe it, but she was the 'smaller man' who dug the knife into Nnamdi with all her might. She is the one of the murderers." She finished breathlessly.

CHAPTER SIXTEEN

Jones and Kings were relaxing in Kings' house.

"You're a marvel." Jones praised him. "How did it ever occur to you?" Kings smiled.

"You remember I told you that Angel to me, was a lady with anxious eyes. I don't look at faces but at the eyes. They can never lie to you, but other parts of the body can. When I requested for a bottle of coke, I realized she was left-handed. Remember that Sophie said that one of the men, the one that did the actual killing used his left hand. But that wasn't the reason why I started suspecting her. It meant nothing to me then, but I always take note of every tiny detail especially during an investigation. I started suspecting something after Sophie's mother's call of alarm. Nobody else knew the story then except Emeka, Jake and Angel, so how could the murderers have known immediately about Sophie and wanted to get rid of her. That was where they started slipping. Secondly, that night at JABO-JABO night club, I recognized Angel as the lady who looked 'familiar' with the golden wig and dark shades". The whole puzzle of the 'wig and shades' suddenly clicked in Jones brain and he then remembered where he had seen it on someone before. "I didn't want to tell you," kings continued. "Moreover, you would've spoilt everything as you were already carried away by the lady's charms." Jones put down his face. "When I recognized her," Kings said, "I was a bit confused because of the disguise. If she hadn't tried to disguise herself it would have been innocent company since she and Jake were both Emeka's friends. No harm in hanging out once in a while. But that was their second slip and that made the suspicion stronger but I still wasn't sure so I suggested us keeping our findings secret, but then unknown to you, I still went to Emeka to tell him about our visit to ATTAMCO. I knew he would pass on the information to his friends. He did just that and suddenly Jake, alias Keneka disappeared into thin air with no trace." He joked.

"But how did you know Jake was Mr Keneka?" Jones asked.

Kings grinned. "Remember you told me that Mr Schechem didn't know who Jake was. It meant Jake was known with another name so I just took a chance: After you told me about your visit to ATTAMCO, I went over to Emeka and revealed everything to him emphasizing when we were going to ATTAMCO again for a visit. I guessed he would pass on the information to Angel who would in turn pass it over to Jake, so when we were told Mr Keneka suddenly took a leave so soon after your visit, it was just as I expected. Of course he knew that once we found out he was Mr Keneka, we would put two and two together. The mistake he made was giving us true facts about Schechem when you put him under pressure with your questions. He was caught unawares and therefore wasn't prepared for those questions so he didn't have the chance to plan what to say and he uttered the first name that popped into his head.

"Did you purposely take Onyeka with you that day?" Jones asked, wondering why such ideas never occurred to him. Anyway, his own part is mainly questioning. He admired Kings intelligence for the umpteenth time.

"Yes. You know he emphasized that he would remember that 'beautiful' face if he sees it again. So my chance came when Emeka confided in me of his fiancee's illness and how she didn't want to visit the hospital. I quickly took that opportunity, but I never reckoned on the young man recognizing Angel that fast. It was marvelous. Just as I planned. Her denial also was a slip on her part. I asked you later if you had heard from Sophie since she also claimed to identify the beautiful face if she ever sees it again. All the stories pointed to one thing: 'The beauty of the face'. In order to be sure, I took Angel's finger prints without her knowledge by deliberately allowing my pocket book to fall on her laps in the guise of apologizing for what happened. Immediately I reached the station, I rushed to the lab to have it checked. It coincided with one of the prints found in Emeka's house. That was when I became sure of myself and decided to find a way of arresting her. We went to the place she called her parents' house to arrest her. The rest, you know....

"What of Nkoli? How did you know she was involved?"

"I started suspecting Nkoli on that very first day we went to Nnamdi's compound for investigation. As you were asking the questions and I was doing my usual observation as well as listening to the answers, I noticed that among all the people in the compound that day, only Sophie and her appeared ill at ease. I later learnt the reason for Sophie's but hers, I couldn't tell so I decided to leave it for the time being. To be frank, I had almost forgotten all about her when she came to us indirectly reporting her involvement in the case without knowing. She also gave me clues that helped in the investigation. Her story meant the murderers were getting uncomfortable and thought that by providing us with another totally different story, they would confuse us, with the hope of removing us from the right path. What they didn't bargain for is that we're more intelligent than them. Just look at the childish stuff they came up with." He sneered.

"But how did you know Angel was in that house on that day?" Jones still wanted to get all the facts.

"Actually, I wasn't sure she was in. I just banked on it from the way that lady blocked us from entering the house. It looked like she was hiding something. I became even more convinced when she lied about Angel having gone to her boy friend's place because I just called Emeka before we set off for her house, so I knew she wasn't there. So I decided that if Angel was really in that house, and on hearing that we called, coupled with the fact that Onyeka has already identified her, she wouldn't want to meet us again, especially in that house if it isn't a family house as she led us to believe. Naturally, she would try to get away from that place and if Jake was hiding there too, they would both try to escape. On the other hand, if he isn't there, she would try to get to him since things were becoming tight for them that committed the crime. 'Partners in crime' you know and 'The guilty being afraid syndrome." He chuckled. "But then when we entered that hotel, I was still uncertain about Jake being there, that was why I told you that if I banged the door on entry, that meant he was there, you should lock it and call for back up immediately."

"Brilliant! Welldone!" Jones exclaimed in admiration. "Without your ideas, this case would still be a puzzle by now."

Kings just smiled. It seemed to be the only thing he's being doing lately since the case had been solved. He always feels satisfied and fulfilled after each successful case. "It's not just me, you also did your own part. It was a combined effort with each person contributing his own talent. That's why we're a team." He told Jones.

"Oh! I pity the barrister. All his world came crumbling when he discovered who his real enemies are." Jones said remembering how Emeka had been called. "The doctor said it would take a long time for him to recover from the shock and be normal again. It was a terrible blow to him, you know. His darling, faultless fiancée. There goes the saying 'All that glitters is not gold'." Kings quoted, feeling sorry for Emeka.

Emeka had been contacted that very night. The time was a quarter past eleven pm. He was told that the murderers had been found. He was watching the late night movie when his phone rang. However the caller asked him to come around in the morning as he might not be able to handle it that night. He had told them he was on his way. He couldn't wait to see those that murdered his brother and why? He quickly switched off the television, changed into a pair of trousers and rushed out to his car. A few minutes later, he was at the police station. Jones met him and tried to prepare him for what he was to meet. "I'll deal with them personally before the law takes over". He kept shouting. "How would you feel if it's the last person you expected that is the murderer?

Jones asked him after they had managed to calm him down and had him sitting. "What's all these?" He looked from Jones to Kings. "You called me here to show me the murderers and you're still asking me questions? I thought question time was over. Where are they please?" he demanded. When it seemed as if they would never get anywhere with him unless he sees the murderers, they decided to take him to their different cells. They took him first to the male's, where Jake was. When he saw Jake, he quickly looked at Jones and Kings, then back at Jake. "What are you doing there Jake?" he finally found his voice. Jake just looked at him briefly, then turned to stare at the wall. Still wondering what on earth was going on? They led him to the female section where Angel was with Nkoli. By now, Emeka was completely bewildered and confused.

"ANGEL!" he screamed on seeing her. "What's going on here? What are you doing there? Who put you there?" He asked, one after the other in his confusion. Turning to the detectives, "I thought you called me here to show me the people who murdered my brother. What are my fiancée doing and Jake doing here? Is this a kind of joke?"

"They: your fiancée and Jake are the murderers, the other ladies are accomplices." Jones quietly explained. Emeka stared at him, then at Angel. Before he could help himself, he had grabbed Jones at the collar, the attendants rushed to drag him away from Jones.

"Don't ever utter such words again." He warned. "My fiancée? Murderer? Have you gone insane?" He looked at Angel again. Something is wrong somewhere. He thought. Why isn't she reacting at all? Why is she so quiet, looking at him with something like pity? Why isn't she crying for him to remove her from that place and sue these people like hell?

"Darling, tell me it's not true." He approached the rail. She didn't respond but put down her face instead. "C'mon dear, I know how you must be feeling. I'm going to get you out of here soon. You only have to defend yourself. Tell me what happened and I'll make sure the person who put you there suffers." He pleaded with her, silently begging for her to start crying, saying she didn't do anything. But why is she looking guilty? Why is she coming close to the metallic barrier as if she wants to say something? Mechanically, he moved towards her too though the metallic barrier separated them.

"Did you do it?" he asked still not believing that she did it.

She nodded her head. "I did it Emy." She said.

Impulsively, he moved away from her. This must be a dream, he thought. What is going on? Angel killed Nnamdi? It can't be. This must be a mistake. What have they done to her? He closed his eyes, then opened it again.

"What did you say?" He looked at her again. Tears suddenly started streaming down her cheeks.

"Please don't hate me Emy. I was desperate."[i] She cried.

"Desperate?" Is that was she said? Oh! The world must be going mad. The heavens are coming down to cover the earth. I'm drowning. Won't someone help me? My own angel, a murderer? Murdered my own brother? Then suddenly, he composed himself again. "Desperate?" he repeated starring at her.

"Yes. I didn't want to lose your love for me. I did it for love, the undying love I have for you." She explained.

"How? Which kind of love would make you kill my brother?" he asked non plussed. I loved this lady, he thought. I must still love her or I wouldn't be here listening to her. He was in a daze. He realized she was talking to him.

"Yes, what did you say?"

"I said it was Jake that talked me into it. Had I known, I wouldn't have listened to him." She said regretfully. "Felicia," she pointed to the other lady. "is Jake's girl friend. They have been together for three years but couldn't wed due to lack of funds for the kind of wedding they wanted. So, when the contract came and Jake thought it was going to be his, they planned on it being a big help in their wedding plans. But suddenly, Nnamdi came from nowhere and got the contract. Felicia thought she wouldn't be able to survive the disappointment. I felt sorry for her and tried to console them. Then I met you, before I knew what was happening, I had fallen in love with you." She smiled bitterly. "You made the world seem so bright. I had never felt that way for any other man. When I realized the feeling was mutual, I was very happy. Finally, I've found my soul mate, I thought. Then I found out you were Nnamdi's brother. You remember the day you showed me Nnamdi's picture. It was a big shock to me but I managed to hide it well so you wouldn't suspect. While I was in England some years back, I had an affair with Nnamdi which didn't end well because he found out I was cheating on him so I knew he was going to spoil things for us. It didn't help to realize you were very close and you practically worshipped him. That was why I avoided the few occasions you tried to make us meet before his death."

She paused. Emeka was by now, beyond shock and yet he wanted to know why? And how? He pinched himself again to make sure he wasn't having a nightmare.

"So how did you kill him?" he asked. He needed to know.

"I became so worried about the dilemma I found myself in that Felicia noticed and asked me what the problem was. You see, we were sharing a flat together. I wasn't living with my parents like I made you believe. I thought I'll explain things later to you, but....." her voice trailed off.

"So.....?" Emeka urged. He had become numb.

"When I confided in Felicia, at first she was sympathetic but I think she and Jake must have discussed it, and then decided that the best way to solve the problems we both had was to eliminate Nnamdi. I know I shrank back with terror after they sold the idea to me. I blatantly refused to commit murder, but Jake kept persuading me until I later had to give in, more so when you kept talking about Nnamdi and how fond of him you were. I knew I didn't stand a chance with you once he doesn't approve of me. After I accepted it, we started making plans and that was how Nkoli got involved. She was supplying us information on Nnamdi's movements in return for the money we were giving her." Emeka glanced at Nkoli who was sitting on the ground with her hand supporting her cheek. She had been sitting in that position ever since he got there." "To be fair to her, she never knew it would involve murder."

"So it was really you that the young doctor saw?" he asked in a daze.

"Yes," she put down her face. "It was me. The other lady was Felicia. We didn't really plan on seeing Nnamdi as he would have recognized me of course even with the make believe 'beauty spot'. We just wanted to put off any trail from us after the murder. Let people believe it had to do with church issue." She explained.

"But you were in London when the murder took place. How were you able to do it?" He still could not place everything together.

"I didn't really travel to London. I deceived you. I'm sorry. There was no wedding. It was all made up." She was going to die anyway so why not confess everything to him. "You nearly spoilt the whole plan when you told me Nnamdi was coming with you to the airport to welcome me. Immediately you gave me that information, I told Jake who called Nnamdi since they were colleagues in the office, and he booked an appointment with him on that Sunday in other to prevent him from coming with you. Jake and I visited him at the appointed time. He was surprised to see us and even recognized me in my disguise. I almost gave up but Jake urged me on. I was the one that dug the knife into him with all my strength." Emeka winced. "We didn't bank on Sophie being present that day, if not, it would never have resulted in this." She sadly sighed.

Emeka stared at her, not recognizing her at all. This woman is a stranger. He thought.

"So, how did you manage to have come out of the plane at the airport?" It now seemed like years ago since that happened.

"Remember, you never really saw me come out of that plane. The plan was for Jake to engage you in conversation while I mingled with the crowd from the plane to make look like I came in with them. Jake didn't know it was you until I pointed you out to him. He felt bad because of the fact that you were school mates. But by then, the deed had been done."

Emeka remembered everything. What a fool they had made of him. Suddenly he hated this woman so much that the feeling seemed to overwhelm and scatter him. Before he knew what he was doing, he rushed at her but instead of reaching her, he grabbed the barrier which separated both of them and started shouting. The cops around rushed and held him to prevent him from harming himself. Suddenly, his hand slackened and he lost consciousness as he fell into their arms. He was rushed to Christendom hospital where he was admitted for severe shock.

"It would be a miracle if he recovers fully from it." The doctor told them. "And if he does, he'll might never be the same again."

"Two big shocks within the same month is too much for one man." Jones commented pityingly.

"This is what I call a Betrayed Trust." Kings concluded as they left the hospital.

EPILOGUE

Angel and Jake were killed by a team of firing squad after they were found guilty of first degree murder and were sentenced to death by firing squad. After Emeka's reaction on listening to Angel, she also blacked out and was revived. She never uttered a word again to anyone, not even to her fellow female accomplices who she was with in the cell, except in the court room where she was tried, until the very day she was to be executed. She was granted a last request: To talk to Jones.

"How is Emeka?" She had asked him when he came. Jones couldn't believe what he was seeing. She looked twenty years older. He felt sorry for her.

"He's still in the hospital." He answered.

"Will he ever recover?"

"We're hoping for a miracle."

"Please, when he recovers which I know he will, for Emeka is a survivor." She grimaced. "Tell him that I'll never rest in my grave until he forgives me; and that he'll always be the love of my life." She made him promise.

Felicia was sentenced to life imprisonment as an accessory to murder. Nkoli, being a juvenile was sentenced to twenty years.

Sophie and Jones got married a year later at Christ the King catholic church IKeja. The wedding was the talk of the town months after.

Kings got promoted to Chief private Investigator. He is in charge of all detective cases in Lagos state.

Emeka recovered, but never got married in his life. He just could not bring himself to trust any other lady after the very one he trusted betrayed him. It's better to be alone. He decided. He ended up a recluse.

THE END